"Don't you threaten me!" Macpherson growled.

"Is that what I'm doing?" Willie asked, smiling with cold eyes. "I don't issue threats. That's for men in Ballinger's line, paid hands that do another's bidding. Me, I speak my mind. I do my own bidding. And I never tolerate a man who shoots children."

Willie turned abruptly and stormed off down the street. He never looked back. He didn't need to. He knew what lay there....

Delamer Westerns by G. Clifton Wisler
Published by Fawcett Gold Medal Books:

STARR'S SHOWDOWN

THE TRIDENT BRAND

PURGATORY

ABREGO CANYON

The Wayward Trail

G. CLIFTON WISLER

FAWCETT GOLD MEDAL • NEW YORK

A Fawcett Gold Medal Book
Published by Ballantine Books
Copyright © 1987 by G. Clifton Wisler

Library of Congress Catalog Card Number: 87-91011

ISBN 0-449-13176-9

Manufactured in the United States of America

First Edition: February 1988

for Eddie Boyle
my uncle, guide and friend

CHAPTER 1

It was spring, but the harsh edge of winter had not entirely passed from the scene. A sharp wind swept down from the Dakotas, sending a shiver across the Kansas plain. Amber seas of buffalo grass mixed with the stunted remnants of last year's cornstalks. Together they swayed to-and-fro at the whimsy of the wind, an ocean of yellow interrupted only by the broad waters of the Arkansas River and the shiny steel rails of the Atchison, Topeka, and Santa Fe Railroad. The first flowed relentlessly eastward toward eventual juncture with the Mississippi. The latter snaked its way west toward the Rockies and the very fringe of civilization.

Not so long ago the tracks had been a distant dream, the faint aspiration of land speculators, eastern bankers, and those desperate gamblers who always lived in that narrowest of worlds between disastrous failure and monumental success. Where once the Cheyenne and Arapaho had hunted and warred, farmers carved the prairie with their sharp plows. Parties of buckskin-clad hunters set out from Dodge City to slaughter the last of the buffalo herds. The Indians themselves withered away on southern reservations or set off northward with their cousins for a final defiant uprising against the whites. Sand Creek and the Washita had finished the Cheyenne south of the Platte.

Willie Delamer knew it, and the knowledge tore at his heart. As he rode the narrow, dusty wagon road west along the river, he couldn't help feeling the world had turned on him. The old, wonderfully free life of the plains tribes and the wayfaring whites who'd shared that freedom was passing. The buffalo were gone, and the grizzlies and elk were vanishing as well. Those high, hidden valleys of the Rockies were feeling the miner's pick, and each year some new railroad opened up virgin country to the greedy, ever-encroaching hands of developers and schemers. There was talk of statehood for Colorado. Custer was in the Dakotas, eager to tame the Sioux as he'd subdued the Cheyenne.

It must be March, Willie told himself as he ran a raw, calloused hand along the neck of Thunder, the proud black stallion that had carried him through another Colorado winter. The cold and the loneliness had turned him melancholy. Otherwise he might not have come down from the high country, ridden through blizzard and torment to reach tne clapboard saloons and ramshackle hotels of Dodge City. And if he hadn't reached Dodge, he never would have known about . . .

"Thar she be, jest up ahead a bit," old Jake Clancy cried, pointing to a faint outline rising from the distant horizon. Kansas was unbearably flat at times, especially in the southwest where even a bare cottonwood proved a welcome sight. The hint of a town, well, that was enough to turn a man to song.

"So that's Edwards," Willie mumbled as he gazed for the first time at an odd collection of plank buildings huddling up to the road. A few months before, Les Cobb had described it as a whistle stop at the A, T & SF line. Now the chorus of hammering workmen busily constructing cattle pens down by the river crossing seemed to rattle the very air.

2

"Got them blamed fools to work again, I see," Clancy grumbled, spitting a mouthful of tobacco juice at the rutted road. "Cow pens and more cow pens. Ain't got a cow left in Texas, I'd bet. No market for buffalo steaks with half of Kansas turned longhorn market."

Willie nodded. He'd known longhorns all his life, and old-timers like Clancy almost as long. Not so many years back it had seemed the buffalo would last forever, that a man with a Sharps rifle could ride the plains as long as the rivers ran. Now the herds were shrinking by the week as band after band of hunters set out to make fortunes from the big woollies.

"Cheyenne say it best," Willie told his shaggy companion. "Nothing lasts long."

"You know the Cheyenne, do you, Wil?"

"As well as a white man can ever know Indians, I suppose."

"There's truth to that," Clancy said, biting off a fresh chaw of tobacco. "Well, you can make yer own way from here, I 'spect. This is as close as I get to towns in the springtime."

Willie nodded, then waved farewell to the old hider.

It's an odd town, Willie thought as he rode between the two parallel lines of buildings. Only the houses on the outskirts of town showed any hint of age. The walls of the shops, eateries, saloons, and even the livery remained raw planks hammered into place. A pair of teenagers slapped yellow paint on a two-story structure near the center of the budding town, and carpenters nailed handpainted signs over a bathhouse next door. Willie rode past them. He stopped when he arrived at a small jailhouse.

Yes, it's odd people who complete a jail even before the paint's dry on the livery, Willie thought. But then Willie appeared more than a little odd himself. There he was, riding a tall black horse like some cavalry general, his clothes a mix of homemade buckskins, buffalo hides, and a broad-brimmed felt hat won from a Dodge City shopkeeper on a wager. A pair of elkhide boots laced halfway up his legs attested to winter in Arapaho country. The long-barreled Winchester in a saddle sleeve and the cold Colt revolver on his right hip hinted that here was a man best left alone.

"Can we help you, fellow?" a shaggy-haired young man in his late teens asked as Willie climbed down from Thunder and tied the reins to a ring on a hitching post.

Willie paused a moment. The boy sat on a bench beside the jailhouse. At his side was an older man with a paunch. Both wore tin-plated stars on cowhide vests.

"You might," Willie answered. "Anywhere about these parts where a man might find work?"

"What manner of work?" the sheriff asked, gazing suspiciously from under a broad-brimmed hat. "Honest work?"

"If it's to be had."

"And if not?" the younger man asked.

"Then it's best known straightaway. It's just midmorning, and a man on a good horse could ride another ten, fifteen miles easy."

"Rufus Macpherson's hiring men down at the pens," the sheriff said, frowning as he pointed toward the cloud of dust rising from the western end of town. "He pays fair."

"Seems strange work, though," Willie observed as he removed his hat and joined the men on the bench. "I saw enough empty pens at Dodge to house a thousand steers."

"Well, Macpherson thinks he can catch the eastbound cattle cars before they get to Dodge, and beat the shippers to Kansas City. That way the buyers'll offer top price here," the sheriff explained. "Says he'll make us all rich."

"And what do you say?" Willie asked, his blazing blue eyes suddenly catching fire as he gazed across the street at a woman escorting her young children toward the schoolhouse.

4

"I say it's foolishness," the sheriff admitted with a laugh. "Mac's got to know we've got a fair place here to live. Farms bring in decent corn crops, and if it's a cattle town that's needed, best set off for Dodge and Wichita. It's like Doc Trent says, we've got the women and little ones to look out for. Let Macpherson build his own town."

"Why do that when he can buy ours?" the younger man grumbled.

"So you expect trouble?" Willie asked, noticing as the sheriff moved slightly that a double-barreled shotgun rested behind the bench.

"I'd say that was our concern, Mr. . . . ."

"Fletcher, Wil Fletcher," Willie told them.

"I'm Tyler Green," the younger man responded, shaking Willie's hand. "Deputy sheriff."

"I'm called Hummel, Walter Hummel," the sheriff added. "Ty's pa was sheriff 'fore I came on. Town kept the boy on as sort of a remembrance."

"What happened to your pa, Ty?" Willie asked.

"Didn't get himself shot, if that's what you're after," Ty explained. "Got bucked off a horse last Fourth of July. Hit his head on a fence post."

"Sorry to hear that," Willie said sadly. "But at least he didn't suffer much, I'd guess. And he left a son to carry on."

Young Ty grinned, and even Hummel appeared to lose some of his suspicion.

"Ever put your hand to carpentry?" Hummel asked.

"Once or twice."

"You might try the hotel. A. C. Wheaton runs the place. Tell him I sent you along. He's got work for an honest man."

"Thanks, Sheriff," Willie said, grabbing his hat and standing. "Maybe I'll be able to return the favor sometime."

"Could be."

Willie walked across the street to where a slightly built, heavily balding man was painting the trim on the front shutters of the two-story building. Willie'd seen enough hotels to spot one, sign or no sign.

"You Wheaton?" he asked the painter.

"I might be," the balding man answered without pausing to look up. "Who'd want him?"

"They call me Wil Fletcher," Willie said. "I've come out from Dodge."

"Oh?"

"I heard there's work hereabouts for a man who isn't afraid to use his hands. The sheriff suggested I speak to you."

"I don't hire strangers."

"Don't see this town could hold a lot of familiar faces. By late spring, early summer you'll have drovers here. Lots of work needs doing."

"I'll get it done. As to the drovers, I wouldn't be so sure they'll come to Edwards. That's far from settled."

"Oh?"

"And if you've come to help with the deciding, I'd caution you that new faces aren't particularly welcome here-abouts."

Willie glanced up and down the street. His brooding eyes caught nary a sign of welcome. Children stepped off into the street so as not to get too close to him. Women frowned and slapped their handbags against their knees. Men glared at the pistol on Willie's hip and the haggard, unshaven face that even when smiling warned of the danger underneath.

"So you have no work?" Willie asked.

"None for you. You might try down at the pens. They're none too particular who they hire on down there."

"No, I don't think I'd feel comfortable there, Mr. Wheaton. Seems to me there are enough pens at Dodge City for all of western Kansas."

"Some'd say so."

"You among 'em?"

"Me and others," Wheaton growled. "You might keep that in mind when Rufe Macpherson takes it into his head to stir up trouble."

"Macpherson?"

"Don't say you haven't heard that name before," Wheaton exclaimed, setting aside the brush long enough to stare hard into Willie's eyes. "He's tried to bring trouble here. We buried the last man to threaten us. There's room in the churchyard for more."

"Always is," Willie remarked as he turned away.

He walked along past the bathhouse, past the mercantile, and on to where he could gaze at the maze of pens sprawling from the railroad siding out toward the distant crossings of the Arkansas. He couldn't help remembering that first time he'd ridden toward Dodge, nudging a tired old nag southward from the Bighorn Mountains. He'd expected Kansas to bring peace then, but it had only brought more death, more darkness. Now he'd come again. Why? Hadn't he learned peace never came?

Once those prairies had been black as Mississippi bottomland with buffalo. Now the land was painted white with bones, the sole reminder of the beasts and the men who'd once hunted them.

What's it to be, Willie? he asked himself. They say there's still solitude to be found up on the Yellowstone. He'd ridden to such places before, so many times he scarcely remembered them all. Often he'd set off into the unknown, bound for nowhere, cast along like a tumbleweed on the wayward wind.

No. There could be no leaving, not now. This time he had a direction. The telegram in his pocket had carried him the ten miles west from Dodge, had snatched him from his hard oaken chair at the back table of the Lone Star Saloon.

His recollection was broken by the sudden arrival of a

7

boy, his bare, bony shoulders scarcely capable of keeping in place the straps of an oversized pair of overalls. The boy slammed against Willie's side, and the two of them rolled into a heap beside a watering trough.

"Sorry, mister," the boy begged, scrambling back toward the street. "I didn't . . . mean to . . . I didn't . . ."

The boy, who might have been as old as twelve, trembled with fear. Alarm filled a pair of watery blue eyes. Three or four companions froze in place near the edge of the road, their eyes equally fixed in terror.

"No harm done, boys," Willie said, getting to his feet and kicking a ball made of rags bound in buckskin back to the youngsters. "Shouldn't you be in school?"

"Just waitin' for Pa to finish at the mercantile," explained the oldest, a lanky fourteen-year-old with strawberry-blond hair falling across his forehead. "Sorry 'bout my brother Rush. He's clumsy to a fault. Me, I'm Roy."

"Well, Roy, it's me that's sorry," Willie told them. "I stopped your game."

The boys grinned, then resumed their contest. Willie turned away and gazed across the street. His heart pounded as he studied the faces of ladies dressed in bonnets, their movements full of grace and purpose. Each time a young one passed, he'd examine her features, searching for a hint of something familiar, a tress of fine, blond hair, a half-forgotten flash of blue in an eye. Perhaps she'd cradle a baby, or lead three small boys along as to a Sunday picnic.

Willie's thoughts were again interrupted, this time by a booming voice.

"Stay clear o' my horse!" a dusty rider bellowed, kicking one of the farm boys away with a boot. "Get off with you, hayseed!"

"We meant no harm," Roy cried, dragging two of the others away to the shelter of a nearby wagon. A fourth was less fortunate.

"Look what I got myself, Reed," a second rider

shouted, snatching the boy and lifting him up onto the saddle. A moment later the rider slapped his horse into a gallop and raced along the street. The boy cried out in anguish as the horseman flung him into the water trough. The street exploded with laughter.

"That'll teach them hayseeds," a third rider declared, climbing off his horse. "Kansas is no country for farmers. We grow cows best here. Let 'em go elsewhere 'fore the hawks pick at their bones."

"You had no call to do that," Roy yelled as he wove his way through the growing crowd to his floundering friend.

"I've got call to do as I like!" the horseman growled, pushing the sputtering boy in the trough beneath the foul water. "I'm Reed Ballinger, and I need no man's leave to talk or ride or spit."

Ballinger's companions joined in the fun. The first grabbed young Roy and pinned him to the ground. The second set off after the two boys cowering beside the wagon.

Don't get involved, a voice whispered through Willie's head. You're supposed to lay low, remain unnoticed. But even then he was starting toward the trough.

"I'd say that was about enough," Willie said, grabbing Ballinger's hand and allowing the terrified, half-drowned boy in the trough a chance to catch his breath.

"Who'd you be to say anything?" Ballinger grumbled, shaking Willie's grip loose.

"Someone who won't tolerate a grown man matching himself up with a wisp of a boy."

The crowd moved back a step or two as Ballinger glared at Willie with coal-black eyes. The gunman's thinning hair and waxed moustache added to his sinister appearance.

"Ben, Zac, looks like we've got a bit of distraction today after all," Ballinger said, waving his companions to his side.

"Oh?" Willie asked sourly.

9

"Mister, don't," Roy pleaded as he shrank back to the safety of a flour barrel. "They'll shoot you sure."

"That's a fact," Ballinger boasted. "Maybe you haven't heard of me. I'm Reed Ballinger. I ride for Rufe Macpherson. These boys are Zac Waller and Ben Tarpley."

"Tarpley?" Willie asked, gazing at the youngster, a blondish man of about twenty-five with deadly gray eyes. "I knew a Tarpley once. Cole, I think his name was."

"My brother," Tarpley said, grinning.

"Yeah, I can see the resemblance," Willie went on. "'Course, I didn't know him well. Only saw him when he was dead. Like you're about to be."

"You talk just fine," Tarpley said, his voice betraying a certain nervousness. "How do you shoot?"

"Better'n your brother," Willie declared.

"Not well enough to live past noon," Ballinger taunted. "I never knew a squaw man who could take three Kansans on the best day he ever had."

"Not three," Wheaton declared, emerging from the crowd with a shotgun. "Only you, Ballinger. These other two show an inclination toward their pistols, I'll scatter 'em halfway to Dodge."

"Wheaton, stay out of this!" Ballinger warned.

"Isn't anybody staying out of anything," another man said, producing a second shotgun. Three or four others appeared as well.

"It's time you left town, I'm thinking," Wheaton said, waving the barrel of his shotgun toward the cattle pens.

Ballinger frowned, then fixed Willie with a hateful gaze.

"We haven't settled with you," Ballinger warned. "There'll be another day."

"I'll be around," Willie answered, his eyes suddenly afire. "Anytime you're eager to find your death."

Ballinger withdrew slowly, then mounted his horse and rode off. Waller and Tarpley followed, their eyes warily

10

gazing at the shotgun barrels that trailed their departing ponies.

"Best you get yourself dried off some, son," Willie said then, helping the shivering farm boy out of the trough. "See you don't catch cold."

"I'll take care of him, mister," Roy volunteered. "He just lives up the way a bit."

The boys collected at the wagon, and Roy trotted along toward the mercantile to fetch his father. Young Rush waved gratefully at Willie. Willie only smiled and shook his head.

"You always put your nose in where it doesn't belong?" Wheaton asked as he relaxed his grip on the shotgun.

"Bad habit of mine," Willie confessed. "Never could stomach the likes of that Ballinger."

"He's shot men, lots of 'em."

"Fast?"

"Bottled lightning. Could be we just saved your life."

"Maybe. Maybe not."

"You look to've pulled a pistol or two in your own time," the hotelman said.

"Not always by choice."

"Could be I was wrong about you, Fletcher. I might have a bit of work for you after all. You can use a hammer, can you?"

"A plane and a square, too. I've built things, though I have to admit of late I've been in a different line of work."

"I'd guess that," Wheaton said, gazing at the Arapaho boots. "What brought you to Edwards?"

"Told you. I heard there was work here."

"There's work in Dodge, too," Wheaton remarked as he led the way back to the hotel. "It must be more than work."

It is, Willie thought as he followed the older man. Much more.

CHAPTER 2

Willie passed the afternoon dabbing yellow paint on the remaining shutters of the hotel. Afterward he stabled Thunder at the livery and carried the blanket roll that contained his scant possessions down the nearly deserted street. Wheaton then led the way to a small room at the top of a darkened stairway on the hotel's second floor.

"This suit you?" Wheaton asked as he opened the door.

Willie glanced inside. The room held a single bed, a small chest, a wardrobe, and two chairs. He nodded, and Wheaton handed over the key. It suits me just fine, Willie thought as he unrolled the blanket on the end of the bed. There was but the one door, and a single window overlooked the back door downstairs. It would be sufficient for a bit of breeze, but scarcely an invitation to ambush.

Yes, Wheaton knows me well enough, Willie told himself. I wear a different name, different clothes, but I can't disguise my eyes, the coldness in my heart. And if Wheaton can recognize it, men like Ballinger will, too.

For better than an hour Willie busied himself stuffing his few belongings in drawers. Assorted shirts and a spare pair of buckskin trousers, some stockings and a nightshirt, a pair of moccasins and some underthings . . . that and the blanket about summed up his life. There was a trunk stashed away at a freight warehouse in Pueblo. It'd been there more than a year now, for Willie'd taken to traveling light.

"Who says I haven't changed?" he asked himself. "Time was I'd drag that trunk everywhere." It had criss-crossed a dozen battlefields from Tennessee and Missis-sippi to Virginia. Even now the tattered regimental flag of the Second Texas nestled with old family mementos in that trunk. There were gold pieces, too, not to mention papers and bank notes representing what to some would be wealth. That trunk tied him to a past, linked him to people and property. It was better left behind.

Not everything could be so easily set aside, though. He took out the telegram and read it again.

NEED YOUR HELP STOP ELLIE IN DANGER STOP L C

A year ago he'd never have gotten that message. After all, Ellie was a world away. But all that had changed. As always when the past seemed at a distance, safely put be-hind, it returned from the shadows to tear at him like the talons of a winter hawk.

Ellen. Even now her name stirred something inside him. She was the girl who'd shared the summer sun back home along the Brazos. There'd been days of racing ponies and splashing their way through the shallows, buff naked and full of what old Yellow Shirt, the Comanche chief, had called "white man's fever." As they'd grown taller, Willie had led her around the floor at many a barn dance. And when war came, she'd bid him farewell with the promise that she'd await his return.

She had, too, he reminded himself. But war changes a man, and the dreams they'd shared at eight, at ten, and at fourteen, could never have been. So Willie Delamer had died at twenty, swallowed by a world of death and dying

13

that even now picked at his bones. He'd adopted a dozen aliases; been Billy Starr on the Cimarron, Billy Cook out on the Purgatory, and now Wil Fletcher in Dodge City and Edwards. All that time he'd remembered her gentle touch, the shining luster of her eyes, the brightness that had been so much absent from his life. And she'd thought him dead.

I am dead to you, Willie thought as he gazed out the window at the distant, deserted Kansas plain. You've wed another, and it's his children you nurse and nurture. They'll be the ones to hear your grandma's stories, to listen to your hymns come Sunday morning.

He dropped his face into his hands and let the terrible silence of the afternoon devour him.

The quiet was broken by a rap on the door.

"Who's there?" Willie asked, fingering the Colt on his hip.

"A friend from Cheyenne country," a familiar voice answered.

Willie unlatched the door and stepped aside as a slender man a few years younger slid inside. Even in the room's faint light the bright tin star on the newcomer's flannel shirt glistened. Deputy U.S. Marshal Lester Cobb had ridden the better part of two days from his post at Hays, and the two old friends clasped hands.

"So, you did get my note. There was no answer," the deputy marshal said, sitting on the edge of the bed.

"I'm the answer," Willie explained. "You expected no other."

"No, to be truthful, I didn't."

"So, it's best you tell me the whole of it, Les."

"And so I will," Les agreed, taking a deep breath. "I told you Ellen married a doctor, remember?"

"Named Trent."

"They left Wise County a few years back, came up to Wichita. Later on Jack settled here."

"Didn't they need doctors anywhere else?"

"Oh, it was my sister's idea, I think. Too many reminders back in Texas. And Jack didn't care much for Wichita. Bit too lively at times. Most of his business turned to cutting lead out of jittery cowboys."

"So they found themselves a quiet, peaceful town."

"Only the peace didn't last."

Never does, Willie thought. I could have told them that.

"Edwards was a fine kind of a town," Les continued. "Jack was made more than welcome. The townsfolk helped build his house, and the farmers saw to it he wasn't in need of anything. He might get paid with a ham or a few eggs instead of bank notes and silver, but I never knew him to complain of it."

"I'm glad she's found a good man. She deserved it."

"But it's a different man she needs just now, Willie. A year back, this Rufus Macpherson came to Edwards. He was a railroad surveyor, but he raised money from Kansas City bankers on the notion he could build a new railhead west of Dodge. He thought to build from scratch, but the best crossing of the Arkansas for fifty miles is right here. Next thing anybody knew, Macpherson was buying title to any scrap of land he could find in and around Edwards. Offered double, sometimes triple the market rate. Bought up shops and such as well."

"I've seen towns bought before."

"Macpherson might've done it here if Jack hadn't stepped in. He'd seen Wichita and Abilene. He served for a time as a surgeon in the war. He didn't want Edwards going the way of those other places. He wanted a town where women and kids were safe to walk the streets. So next thing you know, he's out there organizing those townsfolk he could find to put an end to Macpherson's plans. They passed statutes right and left. No drinking or gambling, no hospitality houses allowed. Macpherson has

15

no hope of drawing trail herds without whiskey and women and gambling."

"Why didn't Macpherson just move his operations out of town? It's been done elsewhere."

"He still needs to ship the steers from the railhead. Anyway, there's a problem with the crossing, too. A farmer owns the spot, and he's determined not to sell. There's fine grazing, and good farmland to boot."

"So this Trent fellow that Ellen married has taken a stand, has he?"

"He holds sway over most of the townsfolk. They back him. The thing is, Macpherson hasn't been idle. He brought in this Ballinger and a dozen toughs to build the cow pens and discourage interference. Jack keeps talking, he'll wind up in Ballinger's sights. It's never been proven, but down in Texas a half-dozen farmers wound up shot the two weeks Reed Ballinger rode the range for the Lazy J."

"I've met Ballinger. He's a man to deal with."

"He's one to keep a weather eye out for, too. If you've met him, he knows you a bit, as well. If he considers you a threat, he won't mind having some fool shoot you from ambush. He sure wouldn't hesitate to shoot Jack."

"You want me to look after Trent?"

"I want you to look after Ellie. To blazes with the others. She's my sister!"

"She's just a memory to me. I haven't seen her in what, eight long years? She probably wouldn't recognize me."

"She was a long time forgetting you, Willie. If you'd been able to forget her, you wouldn't have come."

Willie bit his lip and tried not to let his ashen face betray the truth. He loved her still, in spite of those years or because of them. For Ellen Cobb still held a piece of those lost dreams of his. She remembered that other, better life.

"So what is it exactly you want me to do?" Willie asked. "Deal with Ballinger? He's not so much."

"Don't underestimate him. He's more than capable. It's

16

said he's got cat eyes; he sees through darkness. He shoots best when there's little light."

"Ben Tarpley's with him. I've heard he can shoot."

"So can the other one, Waller. Watch out for yourself."

"I'd better. Nobody else would take on the job."

"I'll do what I can to keep a real clash from breaking out. There's a vote scheduled to decide whether the town will allow cattle within its bounds. They're to decide on when and where whiskey can be sold in the saloons. On gambling, too," Les said.

"I still say the smart thing'd be to get clear of town, Les. Or send Ellie off to safety."

"You don't know Jack Trent. He realizes most of the others can't send their wives off, so he makes a show of keeping his wife with him always. The kids, too."

"It's like Ellie to choose that kind of man."

"It's like her to stand by him, too. That's my worry, that she'll wind up getting herself shot."

"So how do I help?"

"Mostly by doing little. Watch and listen for trouble. As I said, there's to be a vote. Hopefully that'll settle everything. I'm just here to see it's done legal. I might need help. More likely not."

"And after the vote?"

"I've known men like Macpherson myself. He thinks only of his own plan, and he's not one to be put off by anything short of death."

"I've known them, too," Willie said, grimly remembering the range war on the Cimarron, the desperate struggles in the Bighorn country, along the Purgatory, high in the Rockies, and later up in Colorado near Shepherd's Creek. "I learned something down on the Cimarron," Willie added, frowning heavily. "The best way to end a war's to strike the man at the top."

"Shoot Macpherson?"

"There'd be no one to call the shots."

"I can't condone murder, Willie. Not even of a scoundrel like Macpherson," Les said.

"I know that. I'd have a hard time doing it myself. That's the edge the Macphersons of this world have. We give it to them. We play by the rules, and they make their own as they go."

"Or so it seems sometimes," Les admitted.

"So it is."

CHAPTER 3

In those next few days the man calling himself Wil Fletcher got acquainted with the town of Edwards, Kansas. He walked the town from the one-room schoolhouse to the growing cattle pens down by the railroad tracks. Soon he was able to nod politely to the ladies and comment to the men on the lingering winter chill. He avoided the children. There was too much of the lost wonder, the unbridled laughter to their faces. He saw too much of Ellen in the girls, too much of his own former self in boys like Roy and Rush Whitman and their friends.

Wil also avoided Lester Cobb. The deputy marshal was there to ensure a fair vote, and though it was well known he was Ellen Trent's younger brother, he wasn't about to have Macpherson suspect anyone else had been brought to town in case the conflict grew heated.

So far only words were exchanged. Dr. Jackson Trent spoke well and often against the evils of gambling, liquor, and growth.

"Edwards is our home, and we should keep it a place where our wives and children can walk the streets without falling prey to the bullying of gunmen and cowboys," Trent orated, his gaze falling heavily on Reed Ballinger.

19

Macpherson tried less emotional tactics. Great banners were strung from the feed store across the street to the bank, so that even the most casual traveler caught their words.

Men like Ballinger, Waller, and Tarpley exchanged their leather hats and easy-hanging Colts for placards and paper hats, all painted red, white, and blue. Slogans gaily argued, LET RUFE MACPHERSON BRING EDWARDS PROGRESS. Bands beckoned listeners to the new town hall Macpherson had built for the occasion. Tables were spread with roast pork and ham, turkey and chicken, sausages and biscuits. The whiskey flowed freely, and the laughter mixed with subtle persuasion.

"Maybe Mac's got a point," more and more of the townspeople suggested. "It would mean money in our pockets, better homes and schools for our families. Who wouldn't take an easy day tending bar over working fields from sunup to dusk?"

Wil ignored what he could. He'd seen it before, how easy talk held sway over common sense. You fools, he thought, can't you see it's Macpherson who'll feel the coins in his pocket? You'll be the ones to bleed, to huddle in terror, to choke on trail dust and worry over bullets tearing the midnight quiet.

Wil said nothing, though, just labored silently at the hotel. One day he framed a door. Another he nailed boards into place to form a new wall. Half the upstairs rooms still lacked floorboards, and when that was done, there were cabinets and tables to construct, mattresses to stuff, and carpets to spread.

"I never knew a man to work like you, Wil Fletcher,"

20

Wheaton commented when he handed Willie his pay at the conclusion of the first week. "What drives you so?"

"Oh, there's a fine feeling to putting your hands to such work," Wil explained. "Building a place warms a man. Besides, I'd judge you'll need the work done by early June. Texas herds come through about then."

"They may not come here. Macpherson's not won yet."

"I suspect you'd favor him to win, though. A full hotel can fill a man's purse."

"Oh, there are other reasons to stay in my hotel, Fletcher. Families traveling east or west might choose it over the commotion in Dodge City. This is my town as much as it is Jack Trent's, you know. My wife and kids mean as much to me as his to him. The boys were born within a mile of this very room, and my little girl Johnsie lies in the churchyard. A shadow's fallen over Edwards, and I'd like to see it lifted."

"I didn't know you had family."

"My Alice took the boys to Kansas City to visit her mother. They'll stay till things settle down a bit."

"Settle down? I haven't seen much that needs settling."

"You will. I notice you haven't set aside that pistol of yours. My sons Arthur and Clay are of an age to take a hand in what's to come, and I saw too many boys laid low at Chickamauga and Atlanta to wish it for my own."

"You served in the war then?"

"From Donelson and Shiloh till Joe Johnston gave it up in the Carolinas. Finished as a major with the Sixteenth Illinois."

"Federals," Willie grumbled.

"You?"

"I was at Shiloh, too. With the Second Texas."

"A bloody field that was."

"My father fell there. I was barely sixteen. Twelve years have passed since then, and I've yet to know much peace."

"You were sixteen? I judged you older."

"The years have been none too gentle."

"A man can always find a fight if he's inclined to. And yet I've found he can make his peace, too. Half the men in this town fought on one side or the other, but we've mostly laid our grudges to rest. Kansas was a Union state, but she's welcomed Texas beef and Texas cowboys to her breast. We've bridged the split, or so I like to think."

"Yes, I'd say so. Some would give men like Macpherson credit for that. It's his kind built Abilene, then swung the rails along to Ellsworth and Hays. They drove the Atchison line through Newton and Dodge City. Even so, you don't favor Edwards being next."

"Dodge City's close enough. Let the Texans head there. The place has grown fat on the devil's handiwork."

"Why don't you speak up like Trent?" Willie asked.

"Jack's words touch a man's heart. Folks know where I stand. I was there with my shotgun when Ballinger squared off with you. And there were others. Come voting time, we'll stand with Jack. Macpherson knows that."

"You know he's unlikely to be a generous loser."

"Doesn't much matter once he's lost," Wheaton declared. "Be too late then. Now let's get along with our work. We've still got the carpets to spread downstairs."

Willie grinned. There was something reassuring about Wheaton's confidence. But as the voices on the street grew more and more agitated, Wil became concerned. The pistol had returned to Ballinger's hip, and whispered threats began to take the place of roast pork and whiskey.

Macpherson, meanwhile, seemed to vanish. Some said he was busy signing contracts with the railroad for cattle cars. Others said he'd gone to Texas to convince ranchers to swing west from the trail to Dodge. Then, when least expected, Rufus Macpherson himself strode through the twin doors of the hotel and sauntered up to the front desk, Ballinger behind him.

"I'll need three rooms," Macpherson declared. Even as Wheaton pulled keys from their slots above the desk, Macpherson had turned toward Willie.

"I'll take those," Reed Ballinger said, snatching the keys. Macpherson continued onward until he reached the wall where Willie was fashioning a small cabinet.

"You must be Fletcher," Macpherson said in a clear, precise tone.

Willie gazed up in surprise. Macpherson was not at all what he'd expected. He was tall, straight as an arrow, with a rust-colored beard and matching bushy sideburns. His clothes were tailored so that they fit him with scarcely a wrinkle. He spoke softly, but the intensity of his blazing blue eyes filled those words with added power.

"I'm Fletcher," Willie answered.

"I'm Rufe Macpherson. Mac to my friends. Reed told me the two of you had a disagreement of sorts just after you arrived. I hope we haven't gotten off to a bad start."

"Oh?"

"I've got grand plans for Edwards. Perhaps you've heard one of my speeches? There will be work for a talented man like yourself, one who's good with his ... hands."

"I've got a job. One I like."

"I'm certain Mr. Wheaton wouldn't stand in the way of a better offer. I could pay you, I daresay, double, even triple your current wage."

"That seems odd. Are carpenters so hard to come by?"

"Carpenters?" Macpherson asked, grinning. "No, they're common enough. But a man who can handle himself in a tight spot, that's another matter altogether."

"I think you misjudge me, Macpherson. I'm a simple man. I only had words with your friends over the mistreatment of a farm boy."

"I'd like to believe that," Macpherson said, casting his eyes down at the Colt on Willie's hip. "But a simple carpenter doesn't wear a pistol while building a cabinet. I've only known three or four men who'd stand up to Reed, and none of them are still alive. You told young Ben Tarpley you'd seen his brother shot. That was down south on the Cimarron River.

"I've been up and down these rails from St. Louis to Denver, across the Dakotas, through the Rockies, even down to Santa Fe on horseback. I know the measure of a man from the set of his jaw. I rarely misjudge men. You come by that scar painting shutters, did you? Looks Cheyenne to me."

Willie instinctively turned his hand so that the old scar on his wrist was hidden from view.

"Comanche," he told Macpherson.

"I hope to resolve my business here peacefully, Fletcher. I hate the thought of anyone getting hurt. But the thing is, I don't like to lose. I've put my fortune on the line for this town, and I don't plan to see it carried away by some stirred-up doctor and his Sunday-gone-to-meeting neighbors. You think that over. We'll have enough pine left when the pens are built to make a dozen coffins. I'll see one made your size."

"You like to push, too, it appears," Willie said, standing. "Don't make your business my trouble. There are those who've been sorry for such a mistake."

"So, no more pretenses, eh?"

"I never said I wouldn't defend my interests."

"And just what are those?"

"See to it you find out."

Willie left Macpherson to ponder the statement and walked upstairs to his room.

Later that very same day Wil Fletcher made his way down the street to the schoolhouse. Dr. Jackson Trent stood on the top step, speaking to the assembled townspeople concerning the upcoming vote.

"Friends, look around you," Trent thundered. "What do you see? Buildings? A street? Stores, a bank, houses? They don't make a town. Touch the hand of the person next to you. Hold your wives and husbands closely. Kiss your children. Yes, it's we people who make up a town. We're Edwards. All the cattle pens and saloons in Kansas won't change that!

"Macpherson speaks of progress. He tells you your farms will be worth thousands of dollars. He says life will be soft and easy. There'll be silver in your pockets. You'll live in fine houses, and your little ones will go to good schools. Well, friends, what does he think they do now? Look here," Trent went on, kneeling over and lifting a small blond-haired child of five years in his hands. "This is my Billy, and here beside him are his brothers and baby sister."

Willie felt himself shudder as the boy's bright blue eyes glowed with pride and love for the tall man holding him firmly in his strong arms. Then, when Trent introduced Ellen, Willie felt his knees wobble.

"We don't live for the gold or silver men like Macpherson can place in our pockets," Trent told the crowd. "We don't sell the future of our children for a few glasses of watered whiskey and a joint of lamb. I'm proud of this place, my town. I've seen Dodge City and Wichita in their summer madness, the streets alive with gunfire, the singing from the bawdy houses drowning out the hymns on Sunday morning. I took a bullet from the chest of a boy no older than Billy here, shot by a drunken cowboy blowing off steam one Saturday night. That boy died. Could all the silver in the Rockies pay his dear mother for her loss?"

"No!" the assembly yelled.

"Which one of us, dear friends, would be the first to fall victim to such violence? Haven't we already suffered at the hands of Macpherson's bullies? It was only a week ago young Josh Brock was nigh drowned by Reed Ballinger.

Why, Reverend Henshaw's own wife, our dear Sarah, was accosted on the street by a pair of toughs from the stockyards. Haven't we already seen the future Macpherson promises Edwards in these acts? Are we so blind we cannot see where his road will lead us? Stand up with me, friends. Turn your back on this kind of progress. Hold on to what we have, our precious wives and families. Don't surrender to the devil's temptations."

"Sin in haste. Repent in leisure!" an old woman cried out.

"Right you are, Granny," Trent responded. "Let's make our stand, carve our kind of future for Edwards. What do you say, friends?"

"Yes! Yes! Yes!" they shouted, throwing their hats high into the air.

"In closing, let us sing together," Trent declared, setting down his son and gripping Ellen's hand. Reverend Henshaw then stepped forward and directed the singing of a hymn. Afterward the people cheered wildly. A farmer with a trumpet blew a military march, and some of the men paraded down the street, tearing down Macpherson's placards and banners as they went.

"A fair speech, wouldn't you say?" Les Cobb asked Willie as the two of them stood together and watched the mob surge through town.

"I'd say for now they're on his side," Willie observed. "As for tomorrow, who knows? Gold and silver talk well themselves."

"There's truth to that. Come along. It's time you met someone."

Willie held back as Les pointed the way toward the steps of the schoolhouse. A group of women clustered around Jackson Trent even now, their voices shouting encouragement. Les reached back and pulled Willie along. By the time the two men arrived, most of the women had departed for their homes.

"So there you are, Lester," Trent said, gripping his brother-in-law's hand. "We missed you for a time."

"I saw an old friend," Les explained, pushing Willie forward.

Willie glanced nervously up and down the street. Hadn't Les himself urged caution? What madness was this, being seen with Les and the Trents at the same time?

"You must be Mr. Fletcher," the doctor said, shaking Willie's hand. "Roy and Rush sing your praises. It's not any stranger would take up for a few farm boys when it means standing up to Reed Ballinger. You may have had a close call there."

"Might have," Willie agreed.

"I'd like you to meet my wife," Trent declared, turning Willie toward Ellen. "Ellen, this is Mr. Wil Fletcher. He's working for A. C. Wheaton at the hotel."

Ellen stared, her blue eyes suddenly bright with moisture, and Willie noticed her hands trembled as they gripped his own.

"I believe . . . we may . . . have met . . . once before," she stammered. "Long ago, before . . ."

"Before the war," Willie said, clasping her soft hands with his fingers.

"You knew Ellen back in Texas then," Trent said, his voice betraying surprise.

"Yes," Willie admitted. "I was a friend . . . of her brother Travis."

"They served together in the war," Les volunteered.

"Oh," the doctor said, smiling broadly. "I'm surprised you agreed to march with such a beauty back home. I wouldn't have."

"Oh, Jack," she said, abandoning Willie's hands to embrace her husband. "Enough of that. Willie hasn't met the children."

"No, he hasn't," Trent admitted. "Our oldest is William."

27

"We've got the same name," the boy said, shaking Willie's hand lightly. "They call me Willie sometimes, too."

"Yes," Ellen admitted. Her voice wavered, and Willie fought to maintain his own composure.

"This is Cobb," Trent continued, pointing out a smaller boy edging his way past William. "Ellis, you come meet Mr. Fletcher, too. The baby's Anne."

Willie shook hands with the other boys. Sarah Henshaw brought over the baby, and Willie bent over and touched little Anne lightly on the forehead.

"You've a way with children," Mrs. Henshaw commented. "Anne usually squawks at strangers."

"Willie's always had a way with the ladies," Les joked. "But now we've got business to attend."

"Business?" Ellen asked.

"I promised to show him my new horse," Les explained. "I'll see you later, Ellie."

"Don't forget we expect you for dinner," Trent declared. "Come along, too, if you'd like, Mr. Fletcher."

"I'm spoken for already," Willie lied. "Perhaps another time."

"I'll take that as a promise," Ellen said, taking the baby from the minister's wife. "A promise, you hear?"

"Yes," Trent agreed.

Willie didn't answer. Instead he turned and followed Les toward the stable.

CHAPTER 4

"You know trouble's bound to come of that speech," Les told Willie at the stable. "Macpherson can't fail to react to the way the crowd stampeded down the street."

And sure enough, Macpherson did just that. Barely had night fallen than ax-wielding toughs from the stockyards made their own march through Edwards, rattling windows with the ax handles and screaming taunts at the good people of Edwards.

"You folks were mighty brave rippin' Mr. Mac's banners this afternoon!" Reed Ballinger cried. "Why not come out and greet us with the same courage?"

Willie watched as one torch-carrying gang made its way past the houses on the outskirts of town, tossing rocks through windows and throwing empty whiskey bottles against doors. Two sheds were set alight as a warning. Guns were fired off whenever anyone emerged from a house to voice protest.

"I'm going down there," Willie said finally, scrambling into his clothes. Wheaton stopped him at the base of the stairs.

"No point to it, Wil," the hotel owner declared. "No real harm's been done. No one's hurt. Sure, a few panes of glass will need replacing, and a couple of sheds got singed. All in all a small price to pay for the benefits we'll get."

"Benefits?"

"Jack Trent couldn't have painted a better picture of what this town'll become should Macpherson get his way. This just proves it. Men will wake up tomorrow angry. Anger's a good tool to fight fear with."

Willie nodded. Even so he remained downstairs, ready to join the fray should someone challenge Ballinger. No one did.

When morning came, Willie ventured into the street to find Sheriff Hummel and his young deputy surveying the damage. Already boys were collecting broken bottles and discarded torches. John Burns, the owner of the mercantile, was busy replacing three broken window panes.

"What are you going to do about this, Walt?" Burns asked as the sheriff walked by.

"Nothing much to do," Hummel said, shaking his head. "Politics can bring a man's blood to a boil. Best forget about it. Once the vote's over, things'll quiet on down."

"The rock that smashed my window missed little Jenny's crib by no more than a half a foot," Burns argued. "Next time they toss rocks, I'm loading my shotgun."

"That'd be a mistake, John," Hummel said angrily. "Get you, your wife, and the children all killed. I couldn't help you, either."

"You call yourself a sheriff! Why not arrest that Ballinger?"

"Come now, John. You know nobody's been hurt."

"I'm out the cost of a window."

"I already spoke to Mac about that. Those were his boys, and he said he'd make good on the losses. I've got a bond posted in my office. Send me a bill."

"What should I charge for my wife's nightmares, for the little ones being afraid to sleep without a lamp burning?"

"That'll pass. Wait and see."

Willie frowned as he watched Hummel respond in like fashion to others. Only Ty Green seemed alarmed.

"What would you do if you were sheriff?" the young man asked Willie at midday. "Stand up to 'em, I'll bet."

"To thirty drunken men waving axes?" Willie asked, laughing. "A good way to get yourself killed. It'll get worse. Wait and see. Thing to do is organize a night watch. Have five, six men with shotguns ready. That could discourage even a band of drunks."

Hummel preferred to ignore the problem, though. It didn't go away. Nightly, bands of toughs roamed the street. As the final days before the election came and went, the thugs didn't stop at breaking windows and issuing threats. Any man or boy caught out after dark risked a beating, and more than once a bloodied shopkeeper or stable boy crawled homeward in agony following a set-to with Macpherson's rowdies.

As the cattle pens neared completion, the toughs became ever more in evidence. Two or three of them were forever hanging about the hotel. Others haunted the saloons and shops. Occasionally one would fire off a pistol. Each time Willie instinctively dove to the ground and drew his own gun.

"Awful edgy, aren't you, friend?" Zac Waller asked, grinning on one such occasion. "Ain't growing fearful, are you?"

"Should be you getting nervous, Waller," Willie replied. "You and your cronies' days here are numbered. Macpherson's losing this vote. In a week the new laws will be on the books. Then where will you be?"

"Oh, we have our way of dealing with laws."

Willie knew that was true, but he also recalled the silent shopkeepers who'd appeared with shotguns the day Ballinger had squared off with him in the street.

The following morning was Sunday. Les Cobb came to see Willie with a special invitation to church and supper at

Ellen's afterward. Willie was more than a little tempted to accept, but he finally declined. He hadn't been in a church in years, and sitting with Ellen's family would only remind him of how far astray he'd let his life wander. Eating supper with them would be even worse. Seeing her at all brought on a storm of memories, and he found himself shivering from chills worse than any born of a Rocky Mountain winter.

Even so, he rose early. Jack Trent planned a morning rally before services, and Willie couldn't escape a sense of foreboding. By the time he'd dressed and shaved, he could hear a clamor of voices outside the hotel.

"If you ask me, we ought to march on over there and dip that doc's head in a tar barrel!" someone shouted. Willie paused only long enough to fasten on his gun belt before descending the stairs. By that time a dozen toughs from the stockyards were stomping down the street toward the church.

"Wil, the sheriff's gone to tend to them," Wheaton called.

"You figure he'll do a lot of good?" Willie asked. When Wheaton failed to answer, Willie trotted out the door and chased after the boisterous workmen.

"Hold up there!" Ty Green yelled as the thugs passed the schoolhouse. "Put down those ax handles."

"Go back to bed, sonny," their leader answered with a sneer. "We've got as much right as anyone to walk these streets."

Ty started to argue, but one of the toughs reached out and clubbed the young deputy across the forehead. Ty sank into a heap. The others continued on toward the church.

"You all right?" Willie asked as he knelt beside young Green.

"You better go ahead and see there's no trouble, Mr. Fletcher," Ty said, pointing toward the gathering at the church. "I'm just a bit dizzy."

Willie nodded and headed for the church. Trent was speaking loudly and forcefully when the thugs arrived. Instantly the crowd parted, and the burly workers made their way to the crude speaker's stand from which Dr. Jackson Trent addressed the crowd.

"Why don't you mind your own affairs, Doc?" one of the toughs shouted. "Mac's brought us work. He'll make this town grow."

The crowd mumbled nervously as one of the thugs smashed his ax handle against the corner of the stand. Wood splintered, and the stand shuddered beneath the blow. Baby Anne whined, and Ellen drew her boys nearer. Trent only stared hard at his attackers.

"Want some more?" a second tough called, smashing the stand again. A third and a fourth blow followed, and the stand leaned to one side.

"Good Lord," Sarah Henshaw exclaimed. "Help us."

Women retreated, and children cowered behind parents. Only a handful of the men thought to resist, and one of them was quickly clubbed to the ground.

"This is the town Macpherson would make for your children!" Trent shouted. "He'd make your boys and girls afraid to attend church. He'd threaten the women and beat the men. Is that what you want?"

"No," the crowd murmured. Still, the toughs continued to batter the stand. Willie drew out his pistol and in a single motion drove the barrel against the back of the nearest thug's head. The man fell like a rag doll, and a second who tried to respond was jabbed in the ribs.

"Now, the rest of you get clear!" Willie yelled, leveling the pistol. "I've never taken kindly to men who'd torment women and little kids. Give me a chance to use this thing, won't you? It's grown cold with disuse."

"That won't be necessary," Walter Hummel declared, stepping out from the crowd. "These boys have had their fun. It's best you go along home now, boys."

33

"He had no call to draw that pistol," one of them argued.

"I'd say he did," Les Cobb said as he helped his nephews down from the shaken speaker's stand. "They were clearly threatening Dr. Trent and his family."

"Maybe they were. Maybe they weren't. Either way, I'd say we've all had enough excitement for now," the sheriff said.

"They clubbed your own deputy," Willie said angrily.

"Young Ty tends to get carried away a bit sometimes. He'll do with a bit of rest."

"You're a fool, Sheriff, if you think you can look the other way each time trouble trots along."

"I don't know that I like your tone, Fletcher. Could be it's you needs a night or two in the jailhouse."

"Could be I'd be more use there than you would."

The sheriff was livid with rage, and only Les Cobb's intervention prevented Willie's arrest.

"Arrest?" Willie asked Les as the two of them discussed the matter later that afternoon. "He doesn't have the stomach to make an arrest. You'd better get some help down here, Les. There's going to be trouble, the serious kind."

"I wired Thom MacKay. Truth is, I already got my help, Willie. You're it."

"I don't know it'll be enough, Les. Macpherson's making little pretense of obeying the law. Even if the election goes Trent's way, there's no guarantee it'll make a dime's worth of difference. I've seen all this before. It's war. We've got a few clerks with shotguns. Macpherson's got a small army. They're bound to win."

"We'll have to stop them."

"Maybe they'll stop us. Ever consider that?"

"Often. It's why I'm staying at Ellen's."

"You can't fight a dozen men. And if they come for Trent, they won't be carrying ax handles."

"Neither will I."

34

As it happened, it wasn't for Trent or Les that Macpherson's men came. That very night Willie awoke to the sound of splintering wood and shattering glass. Even as he pulled on his pants and stepped into a pair of moccasins, A. C. Wheaton cried out from downstairs.

"No!" Wheaton screamed. "Never!"

Willie drew his Colt from the holster hanging beside his bed and unlatched his door. Slowly, silently he crept down the darkened stairs and into the lobby. Three or four men with flour sacks over their heads broke furniture and scattered glassware. Wheaton pleaded with the outlaws.

"Tell Macpherson I'll never sign away my hotel," Wheaton declared. "No matter what you do, I won't. Now let me be."

"You don't sign, we'll slit you from toe to giblet," one of the masked men threatened. "We know how to do it, too. Lord knows we've carved up everything from pigs to cows in our time. We've watched the way the Cheyenne work at a man, too, cutting away one piece at a time."

"I'll never sign," Wheaton said, trembling as one of the tormentors ran the flat side of a blade across the innkeeper's bare belly.

"That's enough!" Willie shouted, stepping out from the stairwell. His finger drew back the Colt's hammer, and he readied himself to fire at the least provocation.

"Willie, there's one . . ." Wheaton began to say. But Willie heard the footsteps on the stairs behind him first, wheeled, and fired. A masked stranger screamed out in pain as the bullet tore through his chest, exploding through the heart and closing his eyes forever. The shotgun held by the outlaw went off at the same time, sending a shower of plaster and wadding down from the ceiling. Willie rolled across the floor, then fired at a second gunman aiming a rifle from behind the front desk. The bullet caught him in the shoulder. Wheaton knocked the wounded outlaw aside

35

then swung his rifle toward the three outlaws who had yet to flee the hotel.

"Now, let's see who've we caught," Wheaton said, tearing the flour sacks from each head in turn. The dead man and the wounded thug were both familiar. They'd been at the church that morning. The other three were all younger.

"You work for Macpherson, too, do you?" Willie demanded.

"We don't know who we work for," the tallest of the three spoke. "We been down on our luck. This cowboy gave us five dollars in Dodge to ride over here and put a scare in this old man. We didn't bargain on any killing."

"I don't buy that," Willie said angrily. "Who hired you? Describe him!"

"This is a matter for the sheriff," Wheaton said, leaving Willie to guard the prisoners. Soon Wheaton returned with Hummel and young Ty Green. The four survivors of the midnight raid were ushered off to the jailhouse.

"There were others," Willie declared. "I'll go after them."

"It's too dark," the sheriff said, shaking his head. "Besides, they'll only be more of the same. You'll never connect them with anybody in particular."

"The devil, you say," Willie growled. "Whose name is on that paper A.C. was to sign? There's likely a trail leading straight to Macpherson."

"It'll still be there in the morning."

"Not a chance. A dozen riders'll mask any tracks by first light."

"Don't you worry yourself, Fletcher," Hummel ordered. "I know my job, and I'll tend to it. I appreciate you looking out for Mr. Wheaton."

"Sheriff?" Wheaton asked in disbelief.

"If you only had any evidence. As it is, I'd write it off as a prank gotten out of hand."

"Evidence?" Willie cried. "Prank? A man's been killed. Could have been Wheaton and me instead."

"There's not a particle of proof to what you're saying," Hummel argued. "Now get along to bed and let me do the same. Tomorrow's due to be a long day."

Willie shook his head in dismay, but Wheaton pulled him back to the hotel.

"Thanks for your help. I thought I was dead for sure."

"I don't see I did much good. They can just come again tomorrow."

"I'd judge them too prudent to try it again. Not with you around, Wil."

"They'll do something else then. Only way to settle with their likes is to lock them behind bars or dig their graves. Neither is likely to happen with such as Hummel for a sheriff."

"You can't expect a clerk like Walt to tackle Reed Ballinger. He's a fair man to keep the tax rules, and he keeps an eye out for thieves, but Walt's no gun hand. You can't blame him for wanting to stay alive."

"I blame him for what's going to happen next."

"And what's that?"

"Death. Lots of it, too, if Macpherson loses his vote. Won't be anyone safe once he turns his boys loose. He's got no time to mess with more votes or to change laws. He'll buy out those he can. The others he'll chase off their property."

"Some won't go."

"I know that," Willie said, glancing down the street toward the Trent house. "Those'll be the ones to suffer most. That's why Ballinger's here."

The four outlaws were bailed out of jail by late afternoon. Willie watched the quartet ride out of town, knowing

37

they'd never return to face trial or suffer punishment. A great bitterness filled his heart, and he spit the sour taste from his mouth. Law? Justice? Were there ever two words that proved such contradictions?

CHAPTER 5

Election day dawned brightly. There was a hint of spring in the air. Early on, the men of Edwards began lining up outside the door of the town hall. Inside, Lester Cobb prepared ballots as Dr. Jackson Trent and Rufus Macpherson looked on. Wil Fletcher stood just inside the door, reluctantly listening as Les explained the rules of the election.

"We'll count the ballots together," Les explained. "Meanwhile, it'd be a good idea for both of you to watch the polls. That way you'll know things were handled fairly."

"Fine with me," the doctor said. Macpherson only nodded.

"Then let's get it started," Les said, motioning for Willie to open the door.

"That all you need me for?" Willie asked as the first men stepped up to the twin tables and took ballots.

"Actually, I was hoping you might look after Ellie today. Jack and I are tied up in here. I'm not expecting trouble, you understand. Still . . ."

"You can't ever tell," Willie concluded. "You ask a lot."

"I have to. I worry."

"We all do," Trent added, giving Willie a nod. "The

ladies are planning a picnic down at the river. Ellen will take it hard if you don't go with her and the children."

"I'm not much for picnics."

"Go," Les said, grinning. "And keep out of trouble if you can."

Willie stepped outside. Walter Hummel and Ty Green were there, together with a dozen townsmen armed with shotguns.

"I'll have to ask for your Colt, Fletcher," the sheriff said, reaching for the pistol.

"Oh?" Willie asked.

"Call it an election precaution. We've closed down the saloons, and we're keeping the streets clear of firearms."

"You've disarmed Ballinger, have you?"

"We will when he gets to town," Hummel replied a little nervously.

"I tell you what, Sheriff. When you collect Ballinger's pistol, you can have mine."

"I'll have his when I see him," the sheriff declared. "I'll take yours now."

"No, I think not," Willie said, glaring at the lawman. "I don't trust you to stand your ground, Hummel. A man who lets masked bandits stroll right on out of town can hardly be entrusted to face the likes of Reed Ballinger."

"Fletcher!"

"You trust me to carry a shotgun," Wheaton said, slipping in between the two scarlet-faced men. "I'd trust Wil here with my life, and I'd say you can, too."

"You're deputized," Hummel objected.

"Then deputize him, too," Ty Green urged. "If it comes to a fight, I'd want him with us, Walt."

The other deputies murmured their agreement. Hummel frowned, then waved Willie on down the street. Willie could hear the sheriff grumbling. It didn't matter. How could he protect Ellen or anyone else without that Colt?

As it turned out, Ballinger and his cohorts made but one

appearance on Main Street. They came to cast their votes. The remainder of the day they hovered around the stockyards. Although the saloons were closed, jugs of corn whiskey were passed freely. The wind carried echoes of drunken singing, with occasional taunts mixed in. From time to time Ballinger would parade his crew along the fringe of town, screaming threats at the men waiting their turns to vote.

"You don't need new laws!" they cried. "You wouldn't want to make us mad, now would you?"

Willie was glad to be walking away from it all. He arrived at the Trent house as Reverend Henshaw helped Ellen load a wagon with food.

"Good morning, Mr. Fletcher," Ellen said, giving her head a toss so that her long blond hair fell about her slender shoulders. Her eyes were bright as ever, but Willie could detect a certain uneasiness, too.

"Good morning, Mrs. Trent," he answered. "Les asked me to see you to the picnic."

"Isn't Papa coming?" little William asked. "He promised us a story."

"He has to help with the voting," Ellen told the little ones. "Mr. Fletcher's going along, though. Maybe he'll have a story for you."

The children gazed up at Willie, but he only picked up a food basket and set it in the back of the wagon. He'd be no replacement for Jackson Trent. He promised himself that.

"Care to take the reins?" the reverend asked Willie after helping the children pile into the wagon bed.

"Sure," Willie agreed, climbing up onto the seat. Ellen settled in beside him. He instinctively slid a bit to his left. The reverend followed, assisting his wife. Mrs. Henshaw held baby Anne.

"Les said you've been in Colorado of late, Mr. Fletcher," the minister said as the wagon rolled into motion.

"Last two winters. Most recently I've been in Dodge."

"You have the look of a man who's wintered with Indians," Mrs. Henshaw observed. "My brother ran a mission for the Pawnees a few years back."

"I wintered alone," Willie told them. "I've been alone often lately."

"I'm sorry to hear that," Ellen said sadly. "But now you're among friends. Old friends."

Yes, Willie thought as the wagon rumbled along past the outskirts of town and toward the river. Old friends and old memories. Old pain.

Once they crossed the tracks and rolled along to where the others had gathered, the children scrambled out the back. Sarah Henshaw passed the baby over to Ellen, then helped her husband spread blankets out on the grassy hillside overlooking the Arkansas.

Willie walked a short distance away and sat down beneath a tall cottonwood. Below him children laughed and splashed through the shallows of the river. Smaller ones chased each other through the tall grasses. Their high-pitched voices and merry songs tore at Willie's heart. He felt hollow, lifeless—a man somehow walled off from the laughter, the love, the belonging that was life itself.

"What are you doing up here all by yourself?" Ellen asked, joining him beneath the tree.

"Thinking, I guess."

"Come along, take my hand, Willie. Shall we take a turn around the dance floor?"

"I'm not much for dancing."

"You were once."

"Not me. That was someone else, Ellie, a boy killed in the war."

"You came home from the war."

"I came back, but I never came home. It all changed. I didn't belong."

"How could you let me think you were dead?" she

42

asked tearfully. "All this time, and not so much as a word. Didn't you think I'd care?"

"I feared you'd care too much."

"I waited all those years for you to come home from the war. Then you came back, only to leave again on that cattle drive. Les and Trav said you died. What happened?"

"It was my brother Sam," he said sadly. "I thought I could wrestle the ranch away from him. Papa always meant for me to run it. It was my destiny. I never took Sam into consideration. He tried to have me killed."

Ellen put her hand to her throat.

"And what did you do?" she asked.

"I rode away. I couldn't kill my own brother. I've done things I'm not proud of, Ellie. Lots of times. But I never struck down another Delamer. I couldn't do it."

"So you gave up? What changed you so? You were always a fighter. There was a time when you would have fought for me, for the ranch."

"Sam paid a man to kill me."

Willie sat in silence as the words sank in. How could the world be the same when your own brother wanted you dead?

"You had to know I would have gone to you," she whispered. "It never mattered to me where we'd settle."

"It mattered to me. What could we have shared?" he asked, waving toward the children frolicking on the hillside, at the neighbors gathered to share a quiet spring afternoon. "There'd be no quiet house on Main Street, no restful nights and fine bonnets. All those dreams we shared would never be. Ellie, I never stopped long enough to hang up my hat for a year. If I pass six months in the same place, it's a wonder."

"You're a fool, Willie."

"So I've told myself often, but never so much as right now."

She returned his smile, and he glanced off across the

river. She held on to his arm, and something warm and distantly familiar spread through his chest. His heart pounded, and he grasped her hand.

"I've missed you," she told him. "Jack and I named our firstborn for you. I see you when I watch my little Willie race through the buffalo grass. In some ways, he's so much like you. He grins just when I'm most put out, and he has that way of stirring up trouble in the flash of an eye."

"Then at least part of our dream survived the war and the bitter time that followed. I'm glad, Ellie. He's a good man, this doctor of yours."

"He helped me through a bad time. I was sick with despair. I'd lost my heart."

"Does he make you happy?"

"Yes," she said, smiling as a tear trickled down her cheek. "But not like we were."

"It would have changed, Ellie. Everything else did. You don't know me now. I've killed men, lots of them. You shrink back from the likes of Reed Ballinger, but I've been him, colder and darker by half. I've stalked men in the winter snows, and I've waited in ambush for others."

"That was in the war," she objected. "You had to."

"It was after. It was last autumn. How do you think Les found me? Deputy marshals don't ride through Indian camps. I helped his marshal friend trap a band of road agents in Colorado. One we shot was barely fourteen."

"Not you, Willie. Not you."

"Me, and I've done worse. It's best you forget me. My family buried me, and so did you. I'm Wil Fletcher now."

"It's not that simple!" she cried. "The memories run deep."

"I'm sorry for that. In the end I'll hurt you again. I'll ride away, you know. That's what I do best."

"It must have been hard for you to come."

"It was."

44

"But Les asked you. He worries Macpherson will do something to harm Jack. Or me."

"He will if it comes to that."

"So even now you're trying to shield me. Oh, Willie, you *are* a fool! It's time you looked out for yourself, built a future."

"I have no future," he mumbled. "Only the past."

He stood up and took a final look at the children splashing in the river. A wisp of blond hair flew by, chasing a bare-backed boy. That might have been us a while back, Ellie, Willie thought. But that was a different world, and all this remembering is confusing me. I'd best keep my mind sharp, my gaze hard. It's my quick right hand that's needed in Edwards, not the softness you knew when we were young.

"Willie?" Ellen called as he started away from the river. He didn't answer, just continued walking.

After a time he reached a group of wagons. Youngsters in overalls wrestled in the tall grass, and farmers tossed horseshoes. Suddenly a big, burly farmer grabbed Willie's arm and forcefully led him inside.

"I've watched you, mister," the farmer grumbled. "I'd say you've taken a good bit of liberty with Mrs. Trent. And with the doc looking after our interests as he is, too."

"Oh?"

"Might be best if you headed on out of town."

"Best for who?" Willie asked, angrily breaking the man's iron grip. "Why don't you mind your own business?"

"My friends are my business," the farmer growled. "Take that pistol off your hip, and we'll settle this, the two of us, right here and now."

"No, Pa!" a youthful voice cried. Willie's hands were already unfastening the buckle of his gun belt when a towheaded boy raced between them.

"Joshua, stay out of this," the farmer ordered.

"No, Pa," the boy insisted. "You don't understand. This is Mr. Fletcher. He's the one who kept me from drowning. I told you, remember?"

Only now did Willie recognize the boy as the youngster from the water trough. The farmer paled, and Willie paused.

"I offer my apologies, sir," the farmer said, dropping his gaze and his fists. "I find myself in your debt. They say you're acquainted with Marshal Cobb, so I'd guess you know Mrs. Trent as well."

"We grew up together," Willie explained. "I'd not have anyone on earth think ill of her."

"Nor I. I'm Amos Brock," he added, extending a giant hand. "I judge you know my boy, Josh."

"Glad to know we're on the same side," Willie said, smiling as he shook Brock's hand. "I didn't get much of a chance to meet Josh. He was taking a swim in a trough, and I don't think Reed Ballinger was helping him much."

"That Ballinger's the devil."

No, I am, Willie thought as he recalled the confrontation. I would have killed him.

"When you came to town, we mistook you for one of Macpherson's men," Josh explained. "I thought Rush Whitman'd die when he ran into you."

"I don't have much use for Macpherson," Willie said. But as for his men, we're not much different, he thought, glancing at the Colt on his hip.

"You had much call to use that?" Brock asked, following Willie's eyes to the pistol.

"More than I'd care to recollect."

"Before this is finished, you're likely to need it again."

"I know," Willie said grimly. "You have one yourself?"

"Got a fair shotgun and a new Winchester carbine. For shootin' wolves and such. They work fair on the human kind of raiders, too."

"There'll be blood spilled over this," Willie told the farmer. "You people could still stop it. Just let Macpherson ship the cattle, cater to the cowboys, run his card tables and such. Trailing season's a short one. Tend your crops and keep clear."

"That how you got those scars?" Brock asked, pointing to the mark made by a Comanche lance on Willie's forearm.

"I never stepped aside myself," he admitted. "Guess I wouldn't expect another to do it either."

"I feel better knowin' you and the marshal are about. I don't have a lot of faith in Hummel."

Willie laughed. But as he gazed back toward town, the grin left his face. Shotgun-waving shopkeepers might patrol the streets on election day, but farmers firing carbines would never stave off real trouble. A man good with a rifle, and Ballinger was likely just that, would make short work of the whole town. Men would die in Edwards. And it would likely start soon.

CHAPTER 6

The people of Edwards celebrated election night as if it were the Fourth of July. Fireworks shot across the sky, and lanterns lit Main Street from one end to the other. Dr. Jackson Trent stood on the steps of the schoolhouse and proudly announced the results.

"Friends, we've won!" he shouted. "Thirty-two of us have voted in the new laws. Twenty-one were opposed."

Reverend Henshaw led the gathering in a short prayer. Afterward the throng toasted each other with apple cider and sang old camp songs.

At the opposite end of town Rufus Macpherson gathered his men in silence. In their jubilation, few of the shop-keepers and farmers of Edwards had noticed Macpherson's dark, brooding eyes when he'd heard the outcome. Willie had. And when Macpherson promised his companions the vote had decided nothing, Willie'd heard the icy tone of those words, and he knew all too well the sharp edge of their meaning.

Willie slept lightly. The Colt and the Winchester stood loaded and within easy reach. He'd convinced Wheaton to bolt the back door, and Les carried the word to the other merchants.

"Lock up tight, men. Keep a weather eye out for trouble."

After the last of the fireworks fizzled out, that first night after the election proved quiet enough, though. Once a stray cat knocked over a whiskey bottle out back, and the clamor brought Willie to his feet. It proved a welcome relief, for his dreams were full of the Brazos, of childhood and Ellen. Later the old nightmare appeared, the showdown in which he found himself squaring off with a cold-eyed shadow of a figure. Only as pistols were drawn did Willie see, as he always did, that he was facing his very own self.

"We're all of us the same," he mumbled as he rolled out of bed a little before dawn. There's no better or worse of us, he thought. Those of us who survive are cold-hearted killers. Those who care hesitate, and even a momentary delay would often prove the difference.

Willie shared a bit of breakfast with Wheaton, then made his way down the street to the Trent house. Les Cobb greeted him from the porch. A carpetbag rested beside the door. The deputy held a telegram in one hand. He'd be returning to Hays.

"Surely you can stay on a day or two," Willie said, sitting on the steps beside his friend. "You know the worst is sure to come now."

"Can't be helped. I took an oath to keep the law. I'm needed in Hays. Macpherson'll scheme awhile, but he won't buck the law."

"You can't believe that. He hasn't brought in Ballinger and the others for nothing. You think he's built all those pens to collect dust? No, he's tried one kind of persuasion. Now he's bound to try another."

"If it comes to that, you can wire me in Hays," Les said, frowning. "Thom MacKay can always get word to me. I hope there'll be no need."

49

"Me, too, but I've never found trouble too accommodating."

"You'll be here at least. You'll stay till summer?"

"Till I finish my work at the hotel. Who's to say after that?"

"Ellen spoke a lot of you at dinner last night."

"It's best she forget me."

"She won't. You meant too much to her . . . once."

"I know," Willie said, sighing. He looked off into the distance in hope of catching a glimpse of the rising sun. He wanted to leave, ride off toward the Rockies. But, of course, he wouldn't. Not till he was sure she was safe.

"Good morning," Ellen greeted them from the doorway. "Ready for breakfast? Willie, will you join us?"

"I've eaten," he told her. "I only came by to see if you'd had trouble."

"Trouble?" she asked, smiling. "No, we've been just fine."

"Then I guess I'd best get along," Willie said, rising to his feet.

"Nonsense," she objected. "William's gone to gather some eggs. Stay and have a biscuit. I've got some peach jam I put up for company. Come give us an excuse to open it."

He grinned. It was tempting. She read the indecision in his eyes and ushered him inside.

"Have a seat, Mr. Fletcher," Jack Trent said, waving Willie toward an empty chair on the far side of the table. "I'll only be a moment. William's taking an eternity with the eggs today."

"The boy dawdles," Ellen said, grinning. "We never should have named him William. There's something about that name. Jobs just never seem to get done, do they?"

Willie knew the remark was aimed at him. His mother had made the same criticism more than once. Most of the time it was well deserved, the result of some bit of foolishness or another. In the end the work did get done, though.

His recollection was interrupted by the sound of something battering the back door. Willie charged out the front door, then raced around back in time to see two large, muscular men hurl Jack Trent against the woodpile. Logs scattered, and little William cried out in alarm.

"Papa! Papa!"

"I warned you against interfering, Trent!" Rufus Macpherson shouted, snatching the egg basket from the boy's hands. "You've gone and made it harder on the lot of you. I'd bolt my door tight if I was you."

"Hold on there," Les Cobb growled, emerging from the back door to help his brother-in-law rise.

"No, you two listen to me. I will have my way on this account. You can bank on that. You might make it easy, Doc, or you can make it hard. It's your choice, but harm's likely to come of the latter." Macpherson drew an egg from William's basket and cracked it in his bare hand. He then threw the basket down and trampled the eggs beneath his boot.

"Papa?" William cried, cowering behind his father.

"You take care nothing happens to my sister, Macpherson!" Les declared.

"No, it's you should take care, Marshal. It's just a matter of business so far as I'm concerned. Personalities don't figure in. I know my route, and mountains won't get in the way. If they do, I tunnel through them or blast them out of the way. A wise man would see to it that he doesn't become a mountain."

"Oh?" Willie asked, stepping between Trent and Macpherson. Willie continued until the red-haired Scot's bearded chin was no more than inches from his nose. "I've known men who got in my way, too, Macpherson. None of them lived too long."

"I know who you are," Macpherson said, shaking an

51

angry finger in Willie's direction. "Fletcher? That's not what they called you when you shot men down on the Cimarron. That's been a few years now. I'm not sure Reed Ballinger couldn't have taken you then. Reed's had practice since."

"He'll need it," Willie said, never blinking. Macpherson retreated nervously.

"You leave my family alone!" Trent shouted as he recovered his nerve. "Assault's a crime here in Edwards."

"Tell your sheriff," Macpherson said, laughing. "I'm sure he'll have a long talk with me about it."

Macpherson's cronies laughed scornfully, and Willie fixed them with an icy stare.

"Come on, son," Trent said finally, helping William back inside the house. "Forget about the eggs. Mama's got enough."

"For now," Macpherson said, kicking the shattered basket toward the house.

"You're a brave one, battling children," Willie said angrily as Macpherson turned to leave.

"I don't have to be brave," Macpherson answered. "I can hire men to be brave. You, for all your talent with a Colt, can be bought for the price of a few longhorns delivered at Kansas City."

"And you, for all your fine clothes and Yankee bank notes, will die just as quick if a bullet cuts through your heart. You see that you don't make it to my advantage to put one there," Willie said, not with anger, but with a deadly calm that startled Macpherson. "Now get out of here. You don't own this town."

"No," Macpherson admitted. "Not yet."

Willie saw Les Cobb off on the eastbound train an hour later. Even as the passenger cars pulled out ahead of a long line of empty boxcars, Willie heard the drunken rumblings of Ballinger and his comrades down at the empty stockyards. Those pens stood as a reminder of Macpherson's dream. They wouldn't go away, and neither would Macpherson.

As for Ballinger, Waller, and Tarpley, they soon made their presence felt. Nightly for a week, riders darted in and out of town, their faces covered with flour-sack masks, as they hurled stones through windows or tossed buckets of red paint against storefronts.

"Will be your blood next time!" they shouted.

No one slept soundly once the vandals began their nightly raids. Shopkeepers dozed in chairs behind their counters, ready to deal with the intruders. But the riders had an uncanny habit of appearing when least expected. Willie stood watch for them twice himself, all to no avail.

"Why do we have to just sit around and do nothing?" Jack Trent asked. "We know who's sending those men."

Willie told Walt Hummel much the same thing. The sheriff only shook his head and walked away.

"We've got to obey the law, Wil," Ty Green said. "Can't just round up Ballinger's boys with no evidence."

"And if you had the proof?"

"I don't know," Ty admitted. "We'd scarcely be a match for Reed Ballinger. Men would die, you know."

"They will anyway," Willie grumbled. "Wait and see."

Willie had scarcely spoken those words when a shout roused his attention. Down at the far edge of town a young runner stumbled down Main Street, crying out as if a devil were in pursuit.

"Sheriff! Sheriff!" the boy screamed. "They're burnin' us out."

"Get hold of yourself," Hummel said, catching young Joshua Brock with his hands as the boy reached the jailhouse. "Slow down and tell us what's happened."

"It's Macpherson's men," Josh blurted out. "They've set the barn afire."

Willie and Ty helped the boy sit down on the bench, but

53

Josh was clearly eager to return to his home. The boy's face was streaked with a mixture of sweat and smoke. His eyes were wild with fear. Willie gripped Josh's shoulder firmly.

"Don't worry," Willie said. "I'll get my horse. You coming, Sheriff?"

"Where? You don't expect me to go riding off all over the countryside because a half-pint boy runs into town crying wolf, do you?"

Willie only shook his head and trotted toward the livery. By the time he had Thunder saddled and ready, Ty Green was mounted as well. Josh Brock climbed up behind the young deputy, and the threesome prepared to ride to the Brock farm.

"Tyler, you keep out of this!" Hummel called.

"We'll leave that job to you," Willie replied with disdain. "Where I come from, a man helps his neighbors, badge or no badge."

Thunder broke into a hard gallop, and Willie felt like an eagle riding the wind. He was young again, chasing buffalo on the Texas prairie.

He'd never been to the Brock place, but the pillar of smoke rising from the burning barn marked the farm clearly. Ty and Josh were only five yards behind. Willie drew out his Colt and prepared to fire, but by the time he reached the farmhouse, the raiders were well out of view.

"Papa!" Josh cried, climbing off Ty's horse and rushing toward burly Amos Brock. "Papa!"

"Barn's gone," Brock muttered, pointing toward the pile of charred beams and planks that had been the barn. "Seed corn's all gone. Better they took the house. Lord, they've killed the stock."

Willie gazed angrily at the dead pigs and chickens scattered about the farmyard. Two cows lay on the nearby hillside. He couldn't abide such waste.

"Was no way to save it," Brock went on, holding out his

54

huge, blackened hands for the would-be rescuers to see. "I thought I was so strong! Nobody could run Amos Brock off his place. They warned me, Fletcher. They said they'd settle up. Well, they've done it."

"Folks'll pitch in, rebuild the barn," Ty assured the man. "We'll scrape together some spare stock, get you enough seed to plant the fields."

"Why bother?" Brock asked, pulling a trembling Josh over beside him. Mrs. Brock and three smaller children huddled on the porch of the house. "They'll only burn it again. I can't do much good watching the place. I need to be out in the fields. I've got to sleep sometime."

"We'll stop 'em," Ty promised.

"How?" Brock asked. "Ty, you're little more'n a boy yourself. How're you going to deal with the likes of Reed Ballinger? Macpherson made a generous offer. I can buy new land up in the Dakotas, twice the acreage. Sure it'll need clearin', but Josh is growin', and I've started over before."

"But if you all cut and run . . ."

"He's right, Ty," Willie told the young deputy. "You know he is. Take the money, Mr. Brock. Could be the next time they wouldn't stop with burning the barn. You've a family to consider. A man with responsibilites can't always act as his heart bids."

"You understand, Ty. I'm no coward," Brock explained. "But Mary worries, and I . . ."

"I do understand," Ty grumbled. "Somebody's got to make a stand, though."

"Why?" Willie asked. "Give Macpherson his blamed town. Does it matter so much?"

"It does to some," Ty declared. "We voted to keep Edwards a lawful town. That ought to be respected."

"And if tomorrow the folks vote to repeal your new laws? What then, Ty?"

Ty dropped his head. Willie could tell the young man

55

was of a mind to fight. Ty's eyes blazed with determination. He'd be a good ally, this walking scarecrow of a deputy. If Hummel had half the boy's backbone . . .

But the sheriff continued to look the other way. By nightfall Amos Brock had signed over his farm. The next morning the Brocks were on their way northward toward the Dakotas and a fresh start.

Willie watched them go. A bitterness flowed through him. And yet, as he watched Brock hold his wife close and saw the children racing alongside the wagon, Willie felt no pity. Brock was the lucky one. Something fine and wonderful awaited the farmer. It was more than lay ahead for Wil Fletcher or Willie Delamer or whoever he'd become.

Macpherson's next target was John Burns's mercantile. Gunshots announced the raiders' arrival an hour after midnight. Burns's shotgun answered them. A nightmare followed. Willie was still putting on his trousers when the first scream tore through the ebony darkness. A second and a third followed.

"Lord, Clem, are you all right?" Burns called as rifles blazed again. Bullets ate through the thin walls of the mercantile. Cries and screams flooded the air.

"Sell out while you've still got a head, Burns!" a masked rider warned before riding out of town.

As the smoke cleared, Willie joined Ty Green outside what had been the store's front window. Glass lay everywhere. The door was ripped from its hinges. Broken barrels of flour mixed their contents with jars of honey and molasses. Shredded garments fluttered in the early morning breeze. Sprawled out beside the counter were two youngsters, sixteen-year-old Clement and fourteen-year-old Paula. Two smaller children huddled nearby. Mrs. Burns appeared moments later with Jack Trent.

"The girl's dead," Wheaton mumbled, gazing with hatred toward the stockyards. "I say we go down there and put a torch to the place."

"That wouldn't be lawful, would it, Sheriff?" Rufe Macpherson asked as he joined them.

Hummel stammered out half an answer, and Wheaton cursed the old fool.

"What do you say, Wil?" Wheaton said, turning to Willie. "Let's settle accounts. An eye for an eye."

"You best watch yourself," Macpherson warned. "We could wind up diggin' two graves tonight."

Willie drew Wheaton aside. Trent appeared to be in need of help, and Willie dragged the hotel owner into the mercantile.

"Can you find me a splint, Wil?" Trent asked. "The boy's got a shattered leg."

"My girl killed," Burns sobbed. "My boy lamed. God, how could such a thing be? You told us they'd back down, Jack."

"He did not," Willie objected. "He asked if you wanted to see your town turned into another Dodge City."

"Isn't that just what's happened?" Burns asked. "I'm through here, Jack. I'm patching up Clem, and we're leaving, Emma, me, and the little ones. We'll find a place where decent folks can live in peace."

"You have to fight for such a place," Trent argued as Willie placed a pair of short planks beside Clem's injured leg.

"I fought one war," Burns said bitterly. "I haven't got another in me."

"Sheriff, murder's been done here tonight," Trent said as he tightened the bindings. "We'll expect someone to pay for it."

"How am I to find out who it was?" Hummel asked, shrugging his shoulders. "Anybody see the man? They wore masks, didn't they?"

"Their horses didn't," Clem muttered. "I got a good look at 'em."

"Hush," Burns ordered. "We're leavin' this place.

You've got a leg shot to pieces, son, and your sister's lying there dead. You want us all killed?"

Clem spoke no further, and the sheriff had little interest anyway. As the crowd broke up, Jack Trent pulled Willie aside.

"I appreciate you standing with Les and me the other day," the doctor said. "Ellen's told me of you, of course. I should have known from the first you were her Willie. I feel I know you like an old friend from her stories."

"They're likely stretched some."

"If they're half true, you're a man to know," Trent added, clasping Willie's hand. "I don't know what you've done lately or even where you've been for that matter. It's enough that Ellen feels for you. She's a good judge of men's hearts. I guess what I'm trying to say is that if something were to happen to me, I'd like to think . . ."

"Nothing will happen," Willie interrupted. "That's why I've come."

"But if . . ."

"Look, Dr. Trent . . ."

"Call me Jack."

"Jack, if I was half the man Ellie thought I was, I would've come back for her. She remembers a bare-chested boy who was part range mustang and part Comanche buffalo pony. We had dreams. They are a long time buried. I heard your speech. You're the man to make those dreams happen."

"And you?"

"I'm the man to deal with Macpherson. This is my kind of fight now. You may be good at stirring men's hearts, at writing laws and building towns, but I know how to cope with ambushes and raids. Macpherson knows that. So does Ballinger. He knew it that first day when we squared off by the watering trough. I don't hate people, and I'm not greedy. Still, I'll wind up killing men before this is over."

"You just see to it you're not the one who catches the bullet."

Willie nodded. Inside he knew a good gunman never considered losing a possibility. Fear stole a man's edge. The best ones didn't care whether they lived or died. They were tired and angry and drew with the same suddenness that a rattler struck its victims. Wil Fletcher knew. He was one of them.

CHAPTER 7

By the end of April, Ballinger's raiders owned Edwards after dark. Not even the most venturesome of townsfolk dared challenge the masked riders on the deserted streets. Fear and death lurked in the shadows, eager to deal pain and suffering. Heavy oak bolts were installed on doors from one end of town to the other, and winter shutters were left on many windows even though the noonday sun already blazed down on western Kansas.

It pained Willie to watch the sad, angry faces of the women as they escorted their children to the schoolhouse. Ellen's once bright eyes seemed especially clouded. Perhaps it was from fear that her Jack would be the next to feel the jagged edge of Macpherson's greed. It might have been concern for young William, now learning his letters from Sarah Henshaw down at the school. There was another, more painful, possibility, too. She could be worrying about the boy she'd known as Willie Delamer, the long-buried youth who'd taken up the shooter's craft.

It was only fair, Willie told himself sometimes. I worry about her. But Ellen had Jack Trent, the children . . . a life of her own. He, well, he had nothing.

A little after noon on the first sunny Wednesday in May, Willie's attention was drawn to a single wagon lumbering down Main Street. It pulled to a stop outside the mercantile. The place no longer boasted John Burns's neatly painted sign. It was replaced by a cloth banner reading MACPHERSON'S.

"Mark my words," Miles Whitman said as he helped his wife Viola down from the wagon. "Time'll come when this whole town belongs to that Scot. Half the places already do. He's bought out Amos Brock, and we're bound to be next."

"Hush," Mrs. Whitman urged. "Someone'll hear."

Yes, Willie thought as the couple entered the store. Smart people keep such thoughts to themselves these days. Edwards had became a town of ears . . . and eyes . . . and fear.

"Howdy, Mr. Fletcher," young Roy Whitman said to Willie as the boy trotted over with his brother Rush. "Haven't seen you in a time."

"I don't often ride the river road," Willie said, nodding to the boys and sitting on a nearby bench. "How've things been?"

"A trifle lonely since the Brocks took off for the Dakotas," Rush lamented. "I miss Josh. We had some high times, the two of us."

"Well, you've got your brother," Willie told the boy. "Any trouble out your way?"

"Nothin' Pa can't handle," Roy boasted. "That Macpherson knows better'n to tangle with a Whitman. Shoot, Pa did his share of killin' in the war. He fired off a warnin' shot the first time a pair of those bandits came around. They haven't come back. No, sir, they know better."

Willie smiled grimly. He knew otherwise. If Ballinger wanted to put a real scare in the Whitmans, he could do it sure enough.

"You still workin' over to the hotel?" Rush asked. "Makin' shelves?"

"Just about finished there. I've got some chairs still to fix, but the hotel's just about ready."

"Ready for what?" Roy asked.

"For whatever," Willie said, biting his lip. It seemed obvious the first Texas herds would soon be moving across the Nations into Kansas, and Macpherson would draw the buyers to Edwards. Ty Green had read some of the Kansas City telegrams, and Wheaton had half the rooms reserved for one buyer or another.

"Ty says you think we all ought to sell out," Roy said somberly. "You think we can't win?"

"Oh, you might," Willie said, frowning. "But before that happens, there'll be some dying. You sure a piece of land's worth people being killed?"

"It's not the land," Miles Whitman spoke up from the doorway of the mercantile. "It's home. A man like you, Fletcher, could find it hard to believe a few planks and some Kansas sod could mean that much. We grow things, we farmers. We nurture and prod 'em till they yield fruit and grain. Some of us have buried children on this land. We'll not take a few dollars for that!"

"Sounds fine enough," Willie agreed. "I once did a bit of fighting for such a home. By the time I got through fighting, though, the place I knew and the people I loved were all gone."

"We're not marching to Virginia, Fletcher," Whitman said, pulling his boys to his side. "I'll not allow things to change."

You won't? Willie asked himself. You may not have much choice. He'd seen it before, armed raiders riding down homesteaders, herding them onto a hillside and slaughtering whole families with less regard than they'd have for a yearling steer.

"I hope you're right," Willie said finally as he rose to his feet. "Just the same, keep your eyes open."

Whitman nodded, then got the boys busy loading supplies into the back of the wagon. Willie was halfway to the hotel when Reed Ballinger appeared in the street. Waller and Tarpley, as always, were close at hand.

"Well, what d'you know," Ballinger said, grinning as he approached the Whitman wagon. "Seems the farmers got themselves to town."

Willie stopped in his tracks. He turned slowly around and slipped quietly along the wall of the new cafe that stood between the hotel and the mercantile.

"I've got no time to waste with you, Ballinger," Whitman declared, motioning for the boys to hurry up with the loading.

"We've got business to discuss, farmer," Ballinger said, stepping closer. "Rufe Macpherson's made you a fine offer. I'd not pay half so much for that stretch of Kansas prairie."

"I told you before that I don't have plans to sell. I've got corn in the ground."

"Thing about cornstalks is they burn so good," Ballinger said, glancing at his companions. "You ever see corn burn, Zac?"

"Once saw half of Missouri afire," Waller answered with a wicked grin. "Good wind from the west'd take everything short of the river."

"And the stockyards Macpherson's spent half a year buildin'? The town? Fire isn't so particular about what it burns," Whitman said.

"Oh, this fire'd be particular enough," Ballinger said, laughing. "I'd say it'd take the cornfields, maybe your barn. Barns have a bad habit of burning hereabouts."

As Whitman prepared to reply, Waller and Tarpley moved in on the wagon. Taking knives, they slit flour sacks and smashed a keg of molasses against a wheel.

"Stop that!" Whitman yelled, grabbing Waller's arm. Waller wheeled and pinned the farmer against the wagon bed. Roy and Rush hurried to their father's aid, but Ballinger intervened. Tarpley lifted the shredded flour sacks and dusted the boys with white powder.

"Pa!" Rush cried out as Tarpley smeared molasses into the boy's face.

Roy made an attempt to flee, but Ballinger gripped the fourteen-year-old's wrist and flung him against the side of the wagon.

"Miles, stop them!" Viola Whitman screamed from the mercantile.

"It's easily done," Ballinger said, laughing. "Just sign over your place. You'll get its worth and more besides."

"Never," Whitman answered, struggling to escape Waller's grasp.

"You need a little seasoning, too, do you?" Waller asked, sprinkling Whitman's face with flour. Next the gunman opened a jar of honey and dripped the sticky substance onto the helpless farmer's face.

"If I had my gun," Whitman grumbled.

"I can get you one," Ballinger offered.

"No, Pa, that's what he wants!" Roy hollered.

"Tell you what you need, pig farmer, is a good bath," Ballinger said, grabbing Roy and dragging the boy along to the watering trough. Ballinger shoved young Roy's head into the trough, then forced the rest of the boy's body into the water. Roy bobbed to the surface, sputtering and spouting curses.

"Let's make this a family wash," Waller said as he shoved Whitman toward the trough. Though the farmer struggled to resist, Waller managed to force him into the water as well. But when Tarpley wrapped a strong arm around young Rush, Willie could tolerate no more. He leaped out and drove an elbow into Tarpley's back. The

64

gunman staggered backward, and Rush raced off down the street.

"Fetch the sheriff, son!" Whitman yelled.

Tarpley turned to face his attacker, then stepped back as a fiery-eyed Wil Fletcher readied his hand to draw a pistol.

"Stay out of this, Fletcher," Tarpley mumbled. "This is none of your business."

"I'm making it my business."

"That'd be a poor notion," Ballinger warned. "We're only havin' us some fun."

"You're through, right here and now," Willie said angrily. "Let them go."

"Or what?" a deep voice asked from behind Willie's back. The cold steel barrel of a pistol nudged Willie's spine. He turned slowly, cautiously, until he came face-to-face with Rufus Macpherson.

"Now you don't sound so certain who's through, do you?" Ballinger asked, shoving Roy back under the water. "Good time's just beginning."

"Leave him alone!" Whitman shouted, working free of Waller and fending off Ballinger's arms.

Ballinger laughed and prepared to dunk Roy again. He stopped quite suddenly. Willie followed his eyes down the street. Walter Hummel was approaching, a shotgun resting in his weary hands. Ty Green trailed a foot or so behind.

"Don't you get your nose in where it doesn't belong, Sheriff!" Ballinger growled as Whitman helped a coughing Roy out of the trough.

"They're only having a bit of amusement, Walt," Macpherson added.

"That why you've got that pistol in Wil's back?" Ty asked.

"That's my affair," Macpherson said with a scowl. "This fellow was bothering Ben."

"He helped me get away," little Rush explained, popping out from behind Ty. "They hurt Pa. They near drowned Roy!"

"Let the Whitmans go," Hummel ordered as he lifted his shotgun. "Whitman, you'd best collect your family and get clear of this."

"They've destroyed thirty dollars worth of supplies!" Whitman argued.

"Get what they've taken from the mercantile," Hummel said, nodding toward the store. "It's Macpherson's account either way."

"It is," Macpherson said, stepping away from Willie long enough to confront the sheriff. "And it's my place to decide what's done with my goods. Don't make yourself a fatal mistake, Walt. Cross me, and we'll be putting you in a plot down at the churchyard."

"You don't scare us!" Ty declared.

"Hush, Ty," Hummel said, displaying caution.

"Sheriff?" Mrs. Whitman asked from the mercantile.

"Let 'em go!" Hummel said, swinging the shotgun in Ballinger's direction.

"Go ahead and shoot," Ballinger taunted. "That scatter-gun's not got the range to reach me. I've got a rifle that'll make short work of you, Hummel. You old fool! Go back and shuffle some papers. Let us get on with our work."

Hummel prepared to step closer, but Ballinger drew in a flash and fired into the street. The sheriff retreated, and the others laughed in derision.

"Can't anyone do anything?" Viola Whitman cried in frustration.

"I can," Ty said, stepping past Hummel. "I'm not afraid of them."

"You'll wind up dead, boy," the sheriff warned.

"Better that than to stand here and watch, doing nothing."

Ballinger turned toward the young deputy and fired twice rapidly. The first bullet raised a plume of dust just beyond Ty's right toe. The second sliced through Ty's left forearm. The young man grabbed his arm and sank in pain.

"That's enough!" Willie yelled, pulling away from Macpherson and drawing his own Colt. "What's it to be? You want to die, do you, Macpherson?"

"Put that gun away!" Hummel ordered. "There'll be no killing in my town."

"Oh?" Willie asked with wild eyes. "Have you already forgotten the Burns girl? There'll be death and more death until these men are dealt with."

"Put the gun aside, Mr. Fletcher," Rush pleaded. "Pa's over there, and so's Roy. They'll get killed sure."

Willie nodded to the boy, but the Colt remained handy.

"Sheriff?" Rush asked.

Hummel froze. It was all the indecision Macpherson's men needed. Waller and Tarpley swept down like a pair of vultures, tore the shotgun from the sheriff's hands, and forced the bewildered man to the ground.

"Got some flour left for the sheriff?" Ballinger asked.

Macpherson exploded in laughter. The gunmen brought out two more bags of flour and dusted Hummel and Ty Green with the powder. Willie watched in amazement as the humiliated sheriff trembled with fear. Ty's face filled with a mixture of pain and rage.

Whitman paid little attention to the plight of the sheriff and his young deputy. The farmer assisted Roy to the wagon, then called for young Rush to grab what supplies could be dragged from the mercantile. Viola had already taken a sack of flour and various jars. In a matter of minutes Whitman and his family escaped from their distracted tormentors.

"Enjoy our little performance, Fletcher?" Macpherson asked.

"You really think this will solve something?" Willie asked. "You haven't won anything today. You've sown the seeds of death."

"Oh?" Macpherson said, laughing loudly.

"Yes," Willie said, glaring. "There'll be a price paid for this day's work. I expect you'll be the one who pays it, too."

"Don't you threaten me!" Macpherson growled.

"Is that what I'm doing?" Willie asked, smiling with cold eyes. "I don't issue threats. That's for men in Ballinger's line, paid hands that do another's bidding. Me, I speak my mind. I do my own bidding. And I never tolerate a man who shoots children."

Willie turned abruptly and stormed off down the street. He never looked back. He didn't need to. He knew what lay there.

CHAPTER 8

By late afternoon word of Hummel's humiliation had spread through Edwards like wildfire. Women gathered at the church to pray for salvation. The men collected at the livery to discuss the problem. Willie left the townspeople to talk and pray. He had work to do.

"You can leave that for a time," Wheaton said as Willie sanded the rough pine shelves of a new bookcase he was building behind the front desk of the hotel. "We've got trouble."

"Oh?"

"Jack Trent's called a town meeting. Thought you might care to come along."

"I'm not much for meetings, you know. I think that's your calling; yours, the preacher's, and Dr. Trent's."

"Just now we might have more need of your services than anybody's."

Yes, Willie thought, reluctantly setting aside his work and following the hotel owner to the door.

The meeting was held in the church. Willie was amazed to find half the county crowded into the little one-room chapel. Children lined both edges of the steps. Their mothers and fathers grumbled and fretted. Jack Trent huddled with Reverend Henshaw beside the pulpit. Wheaton joined them. Willie sat on the corner of a bench next to young Ty Green.

"Folks, let's quiet down just a bit," the reverend finally said. "You know we've had some trouble of late. Jack and I thought we ought to gather our thoughts and come up with a plan of action. To begin with, Walt Hummel's asked to speak to us."

The crowd mumbled under its breath as the sheriff made his way to the pulpit. The people were clearly displeased. Hummel made no effort to apologize for his failures. Instead he took a different tack.

"Friends, you know I agreed to serve you as sheriff better'n two years back when Ty's pa got himself killed. But we were just a church, a mercantile store, and a few farms back then. Now this place is a real town. I never bargained takin' on the likes of Reed Ballinger. I've got no gift for gunplay. I don't need a job so bad that I'm willin' to get myself shot over it."

Hummel then removed the sheriff's badge from his vest and handed it over to the reverend.

"Walt?" Trent asked.

"Sorry, Doc, but I've said all there is to say. I can't stop Ballinger. You all saw that. I'd be a fool to try. Find yourself a man who can, or one who's willin' to try at least. Me, I'm leavin' town."

"Good riddance," a woman in the back of the church remarked.

"Coward," another grumbled.

"Well, I'm no coward!" Ty Green cried, rising to his feet. His left forearm was heavily bandaged. "I'll do my duty. If it's a sheriff you want . . ."

"Ty, hold on there," Trent called, making his way from the pulpit down the aisle until he reached young Green.

"My pa was sheriff," Ty went on, speaking to the crowd

in an emotion-filled voice. "He stood for law, and he didn't back down to anybody. Neither will I!"

"We know," Trent answered, clasping the young man about the shoulders. "You've got all the heart in the world, son, but facing a man like Ballinger's a task for an experienced man. You'd only get yourself killed."

"I could help such a man," Ty said, glancing at Willie. "Wil Fletcher's not backed down from Ballinger. He's stood up to the lot of 'em twice."

"I'm no sheriff," Willie muttered. "I've got a job."

"We're sure A.C. would absolve you from any responsibility to him if you were to take up a badge," Trent said, glancing at Wheaton. The innkeeper nodded. Willie frowned and shook his head.

"Then what's to be done?" Reverend Henshaw asked. "We need help. Shall we send to Dodge? Maybe . . ."

"Hire a Ballinger ourselves?" Trent asked. "That'd make us no better than Macpherson and Ballinger."

"You'll not find a man there you can pay to face Macpherson," Willie told them. "You won't pay the price it'd take. No, you'll not win fighting Macpherson on his terms."

"I'll wire my brother-in-law," Trent declared. "Les Cobb. He's a deputy U.S. marshal. He'll know what to do. Could be he'll even come himself. Surely we can match a marshal's salary amongst us."

The group voiced their agreement. Wille nodded. It did seem the only practical course of action.

"Now, in the meantime, we ought to get ourselves organized," Trent began. "No need for a thing like what happened today being repeated. We won't stand for such conduct. It's time we deputized a dozen men, put them on the streets with shotguns."

"And just which dozen do we need to make coffins for?" asked a deep voice from the doorway. Willie watched with interest as Zac Waller strolled inside leading a dozen toughs from the stockyards. Ballinger then appeared, a sinister smile on his lips.

"You bunch of old crows!" Ballinger shouted, upsetting the back bench so that people spilled onto the floor. "Get out! What do you mean to be doing? You're finished here, just like that so-called sheriff who's gone racing out of town on the fastest horse to be found. I'm the law here now! I make the rules. Those who don't like it best step forward here and now."

One or two started to speak, but Waller's men forced them back into their seats. The reverend raised his voice in protest. A burly cowboy knocked the minister to the floor. Trent rushed to the preacher's side. Only Willie and Ty Green managed to rise without paying a price.

"I think you'd best leave, Ballinger," Willie said at last. "You're not welcome here."

"Are you?" Ballinger asked, laughing. "In a church? Fletcher, I can't think of a less likely place for us to meet. I hear you're fast. You killed men down on the Cimarron, or so it's said. Well, I've shot my share as well."

"Difference is that I always looked mine in the eye," Willie said, staring coldly at the killers. "Now why don't you leave these people to their business. You've made your point. We know you're about."

"I go when I choose," Ballinger growled. "I do as I please."

"You go and do as Macpherson bids. We all know that. Now go back and tell that red-haired son of Satan we're still here, too. He's not scared everyone out of the county. You've still got work ahead of you."

"For which I'm well paid."

"I hope so. Time may be coming when you'll wonder about that."

Willie's eyes now blazed fiercely, and his fingers nervously flirted with the handle of his pistol. Ballinger nodded for his cronies to withdraw. They did so, upsetting furniture and knocking people about as they went.

"You sure you won't accept a badge, Mr. Fletcher?" Mrs. Henshaw asked. "It seems to me you're making a common cause with us."

"I'm no lawman," Willie said, declining the badge. "But I'm no one to stand aside when people are pushed around, either."

Mrs. Henshaw wasn't the sole woman to raise the issue with Wil Fletcher. As he departed the church, a small hand grabbed his elbow.

"Mr. Fletcher," William Trent spoke in his high-pitched voice, "Mama would like to see you."

"Oh?" Willie asked, studying the boy's trembling hands.

"She told me to ask you to wait for her."

Willie nodded, then made his way through the throng toward the schoolhouse. Ellen appeared shortly thereafter, holding baby Anne in her hands and leading little Ellis and Cobb along beside her.

"William, see to the baby a moment, won't you?" she asked, passing Anne to her brother. "Go along with Will, boys. I'll just be a moment."

"Yes'm," the boys replied obediently.

"And what am I to do?" Willie asked as the little ones continued down the street.

"What you can," she said, smiling sadly. "You won't take the badge, will you?"

"No," he mumbled.

"Why not? Les wears one."

"I've got no faith in badges and laws and such," Willie told her. "They're only a ruse to hide behind."

"You don't believe that!"

"I do. I've seen it all before. It was a judge back in Palo Pinto that robbed us blind, wasn't it? Later he helped Sam steal half the county. Didn't your own father lose his place? Out here men can buy the law like they buy flour and beans. Once the people decided matters, but that all changed with the war. Now the rich and powerful run things. The rest of us get by as we can."

"You really have changed. The man I used to know would have ridden through hell to help a friend."

"I came here, didn't I?"

"When will you leave?"

"When I'm sure you're safe," he said, eyeing the children. "That much I promised myself."

"Why, Willie? It's been so long . . . What can you hope to accomplish?"

"Maybe nothing."

"I don't believe that. You remember, too, don't you? You're still trying to believe in something . . . the law, the truth, something. Has life hurt you so badly?"

"Never so much as when I watch you and the children, Ellie. I can't help wondering what we might have had."

"I know."

"It'd be real easy for me to let Trent get himself killed in all this. He's bound to be the target sooner or later. He's holding these folks together, and Macpherson can't abide that."

"Jack's a good man."

"He loves you. That's clear."

"And I love him."

"Once you loved me."

"I still do, Willie," she said, grasping his hands. "Can you understand how I can feel for two men at the same time?"

"No, but I read it in your eyes."

"I pray Jack will be safe, but I worry more for you. You've never been cautious in your whole life, Willie. You're going to rush into something one of these days and get yourself shot to pieces. It could happen here."

"It could, but it won't. That'd be the easy way out for me, Ellie. Life never dealt me an easy hand, so it's not apt to start now. No, I just go on, no better and no worse."

"It's not what I'd wish for you, darling Willie," she said, gripping his hands tightly.

Nor I, he thought as he broke away from her grasp. But it's what's destined to be.

The two days that followed proved difficult for Willie. He did his best to keep out of sight. There was plenty to do at the hotel, especially when Wheaton decided to place bolts on all the doors.

"I used to be a trusting man," Wheaton told Willie, "but I've learned caution. I keep my shotgun handy now, too."

"That's wise. I'd say Macpherson could still use a hotel."

Wheaton nodded. The innkeeper understood all too well what it meant to hold property coveted by Rufus Macpherson. But when riders came calling at the hotel, they proved to be quite welcome. Ty Green ushered in Les Cobb.

"So, you've traded in your marshal's star for a sheriff's badge," Willie observed. "Got a deputy and all."

"A fair man on horseback, this youngster," Les said, slapping Ty on the back. "How about tending the animals, Ty? I've got some business to discuss with Mr. Fletcher here."

"Oh?" Willie asked after Ty left. "Not offering me a badge, are you?"

"I need help, Willie. You know that. Ty's got the nerve to be a good man in time. He needs seasoning. You and I could give him time to grow."

"I've got a job."

"Can you really sit here building cabinets and framing windows when people are being robbed and killed by the likes of Rufe Macpherson? You know it's like back home on the Brazos. Your brother Sam did the same thing. You just stood by then, too."

"It's not in me, Les."

"Not in you? Ty tells me you've stood up to Ballinger. I know you better than you know yourself. When he threatens Ellie, you'll stand with us. Why not put on this badge and help me prevent that?"

"No, Les."

"Why not?"

"Because that badge won't make me any better than I am. What you, what this town wants is my Colt, not me. You want me with you because I can deal death, fast and cold and heartless. You saw me do it out in Colorado. I'd done it a hundred times before, each time dying a little inside. But I never did it hiding behind a hunk of tin. Besides, I can do things operating on my own you'll never do."

"I wired Thom MacKay. He'll come in time."

"Then maybe you won't need me."

"Ballinger, Waller, Tarpley . . . not to mention the dozen or so stockyard hands Macpherson's signed on. Not very good odds, my friend."

"No," Willie agreed. "Why not talk Trent into leaving? You might succeed. Les, people will get killed here. Some already have. For what? A few hills and a stretch of prairie?"

"There was a time when you would have fought the world over a piece of land straddling the Brazos."

"A time long past."

"Can you have changed that much?"

"Maybe not. Truth is, I'll likely wind up shooting down Ballinger in that street out there. Or you will. Or he'll shoot us. It'd be better if there was another way."

"There is. Macpherson can find himself another town."

"He won't."

"And Jack won't leave. That's what it comes down to."

"I know," Willie mumbled. "I know."

No sooner had Les left than the red-haired Scot appeared.

"I'd like a moment of your time, Mr. Fletcher," Macpherson said as Willie fitted a shelf in its place behind the front desk.

"I'm busy," Willie replied.

"We are, too," Ballinger said, slipping inside the door. The few people gathered in the lobby of the hotel left hurriedly. Willie reluctantly joined Macpherson at a nearby table.

"I'll come straight to the point, Fletcher," Macpherson said, taking a thick roll of bank notes from his coat. "I'm here to offer you a generous salary to come to work for me. I've got a thousand dollars here to get your attention. There's an extra hundred a week for you."

"That's a lot of money, especially when you've already hired some expensive talent."

Willie eyed Ballinger. Macpherson merely smiled.

"Some might say it was an unnecessary expense, but time's short. The first herds up from Texas will be here soon. Could be you might take Reed, though I doubt it. If so, Zac or Tarpley would finish you off, but they could wind up worse for the effort. That would set me back. It'd be an inconvenience, one I'm able to avoid perhaps."

"I don't sell my gun."

"You did once. You rode with Mike Dunstan on the Cimarron. I know enough of your history to know you're no saint, Fletcher."

"I never took a hand in beating kids or shooting girls."

"You won't have to now, either. Just keep the new sheriff busy. He needn't even know you're taking my pay."

"I won't be. Find yourself another man, Macpherson."

"I have. Several. Listen closely now, Fletcher. I'm no man to turn down. Those who aren't with me are against me."

"I'll never be with you. I know you, Macpherson, better than you might think. I've known your kind all my life. You're the shadow that falls across the sun, that shuts out the warmth and the laughter. You're like a plague."

"I am to my enemies."

"Keep this in mind, though. I can be just as dark, as sudden and deadly myself. If you know who I am and where I've been, then you know men who've considered themselves fast have tried me before. They're all dead, Macpherson. They weren't fast enough."

"They weren't Reed Ballinger, either," Ballinger said, laughing from the doorway. "You pick the time, Fletcher. We'll see."

"Pick yourself out one of those fine carved headstones," Willie answered coldly. "Wouldn't want you thrown into a shallow grave marked with a plank."

Ballinger's eyes lit, and his face reddened. Macpherson waved the gunman outside, though.

"We'll meet again, Fletcher," Macpherson said as he left. "Be sure of that."

Willie nodded grimly, then resumed his work.

Later on that evening Ty Green showed up at the hotel to share dinner. Afterward, Willie and the young deputy made night rounds together.

"For better or worse, you're on our side now," Ty whispered. "Everybody in town heard about Macpherson's offer and how you turned it down. We're glad of your help, Les and me."

"I'm not looking to wind up in the middle of another war, Ty," Willie explained. "There'll be no glory in this thing, only cold and lonely death."

"Aren't there things worth dying for, Wil?"

"I used to think so, but once you've seen hundreds, thousands even, fall, each in turn, you begin to wonder. What difference can one man ever make anyway?"

"A little, I figure."

"Very little, Ty. Very little indeed."

"I don't believe that."

No, Willie thought, recalling how at sixteen he'd braved the rifle fire at Shiloh a dozen times. You're young, Ty, and you'll learn. Maybe. If they don't kill you first.

CHAPTER 9

The arrival of Lester Cobb did little to halt the midnight terror that swept across Edwards, Kansas. The second night after Les had pinned on the sheriff's badge, a gang of toughs from the cowpens gathered at the saloon, drinking and boasting and firing off pistols into the air. Soon bands of armed men paraded down Main Street, smashing windows and shattering whiskey bottles against doors. Even the mildest protest brought a storm of curses in answer, and those few men who had the courage to step out into the night were greeted with heavy blows from fists and clubs. In no time at all the air filled with a mixture of men's groans and children's cries.

Willie did his best to ignore it all. He knew it was Ballinger's bait, an attempt to lure Cobb or Wil Fletcher out into the open where a shot from cover might be muffled by the confusion.

I know your game well, Ballinger, Willie thought as he twirled the cylinder of his Colt. He'd oiled the gun until the action was smooth as goose down. The Winchester rested against the wall a foot away, its magazine full and ready.

"Wil, you'd best come help," Ty Green suddenly cried out from the corridor. "Wil?"

The young deputy banged his fists on Willie's door. Slowly, cautiously, Willie eased six bullets into the empty chambers of the pistol, then slid the Colt into its holster. He cradled the Winchester in his hands then and started for the door. It opened with a shrill whine.

Willie half expected to find Reed Ballinger holding a gun to Ty's head. But as it happened, Ty stood alone, a pale, worried figure half hidden by the dim passageway.

"What's the matter?" Willie asked.

"Trouble. They're getting pretty wild. The whiskey's talking. Those fellows say Dr. Trent's the cause of all their problems."

"Oh?"

"Seems Macpherson's told 'em to leave. There'll be no herds pulling into Edwards after all, no jobs or money. They're in a bad temper, those men. Said they ought to string old Trent up by the church steeple so all the people could get a good look at the reason Edwards died."

"Idle talk."

"One of 'em had a rope."

Willie frowned. He hadn't bargained on this.

"Where's Les?" he asked.

"Out havin' a look around. You figure we ought to check on the Trent place?"

"Yes," Willie said, sighing. "You stay a step ahead of me, Ty. I yell, you drop. Understand?"

"You expectin' a bushwhack?"

"It'd seem the night for it. Come on. Let's have ourselves a good look."

Willie led the way downstairs, then slipped silently through the narrow hallway and on through the back door. Once outside, he motioned for Ty to hug the side of the darkened hotel. Safely in the shadows, the two of them were less likely to attract attention.

"I don't much care for this," Ty muttered as Willie slid past him and continued along the murky backs of the cafe and mercantile. Piles of garbage awaiting burning lay like silent traps to ensnarl their feet. Pools of water and refuse lurked here and there. Willie's feet seemed to have eyes, but Ty managed to stumble over each obstacle.

"Do you hear them?" the deputy asked. "Just down the street?"

Willie frowned. The singing had given way to angry shouts. A new voice joined the argument. It belonged to Jack Trent. Up ahead a child shrieked. Willie bit his lip and hurried his pace.

"I wish we were out in the street," Ty said as Willie broke into a run.

No, this is better, Willie thought as he darted from house to house, fixing in his mind the size of the crowd, the location of the leaders, the possible escape routes. He'd done it before. It was familiar, comfortable, this night fighting. It wasn't so different from raiding Yank supply depots back in Virginia. Hit hard and run fast. That had been the secret then. But this was no raid, he reminded himself. He'd come to shield Ellen, to protect her family.

Willie made a final dash to the privy. The stable was only a few feet distant. Ahead he could see lanterns burning brightly inside the house. Jack Trent stood beside Les Cobb on the porch. The two men gestured wildly at an encircling crowd of drunken stockmen. In the shadows of the stable a pair of men hid, each steadying a carbine in jittery hands.

"Wil?" a weary Ty Green asked as he gasped for breath. "Why'd you stop?"

"Shhh, you fool," Willie whispered, pointing toward the shadowy figures hiding in the stable. "We've got work to do."

Ty nodded, and Willie pointed toward the back door of the house. The deputy nodded again, then made his way there. Willie crawled through the high grass toward the stable itself. As the first of the ambushers leveled a carbine at the house, Willie sprang forward. With all the sudden force he could manage, Willie swung the barrel of his Winchester until it slammed the gunman across the forehead. The would-be bushwhacker collapsed in a heap, and his companion raced off in panic.

Two shots rang out from across the street. The first splintered the side of the stable only inches from Willie's left hand. The second smashed a window in the front of the house. A child screamed. Willie raised his rifle, fixed the fleeing gunman in his sights and fired. The bullet tore through the man's back, and he dropped instantly to the ground.

"Who's shootin'?" one of the crowd called out. "Lord, you almost took off my ear!"

"Hold your fire!" another pleaded.

"They're after Trent!" a third yelled. "Let's get out of here."

The throng nervously scattered as more shots split the charcoal night. Willie could tell from the flashes that someone was shooting from maybe a hundred yards straight ahead. Trent crawled through the door and sought refuge inside. Les crept in the opposite direction, then raced forward until he reached the shelter of a watering trough.

"You all right, Wil?" Ty hollered from the back door.

"Get down!" Willie yelled as the slender deputy stepped into the doorway. His figure was outlined by the light of a lantern inside the house. Ty ducked only seconds before the door exploded with gunfire.

"You over there, Willie?" Les called. "Can you see where it's coming from?"

"Just ahead and a bit to your right," Willie answered. "I

got one and knocked a second senseless. I think there are a pair left, though."

"I count two, maybe three," Les grumbled. "Think we ought to go after 'em?"

Willie didn't bother answering. Leaving bushwhackers standing was inviting a repeat performance. By now the drunken stockmen had returned up the street. Stalking a pair of sharpshooters was old hat. The darkness that might have been their shield was Willie's second home.

There's no escaping, he silently told the gunmen. We'll soon see how you like being the target.

Willie crawled forward, his ears ever alert for the slightest sound. By the time he reached Les Cobb, Willie had located the first of the shooters.

"One's just back of that house across the street," Willie whispered as he readied himself for the dangerous approach. "The other's likely up the street a bit, maybe hiding in a house."

"I thought I heard somebody moving in the Phelps's wagon. It's maybe two hundred yards to the right."

"A good spot for a shooter. Let's see if we can't get the one on the left first."

"Sure."

Willie turned toward the house and shouted, "Douse the lights there, Ty! Let's even up the odds some."

The gunman at the wagon responded with a pair of rapid shots. Neither came very close. The lanterns flickered, then swallowed their flames. The children inside whined in terror as the rifles across the street opened fire. With only the faint outline of the house as a target, though, the bullets had little chance of hitting anyone.

Willie, meanwhile, crept off to his left. Darkness was an old friend. He was at home in the eerie shadows of the night. And as he began to pick out the outline of a rifleman from the dim lines of the house, he smiled.

You're finished, he said, silently preparing to fire. Something stopped him. It wasn't compassion. But it did little good to shoot such desperate hirelings. Better to bring them to jail, get some answers. Maybe Les was right. Perhaps the law could put Macpherson in his place.

"That you, Reed?" the gunman called out as Willie crept nearer.

"Just your luck it's not," Willie said, ramming the barrel of his Winchester into the bushwhacker's ribs. "Drop that rifle before I send your insides to Colorado!"

"Reed!" the frightened ambusher managed to bawl before Willie decked him.

"I've got this one, Les," Willie shouted. "Ready to set off after the others?"

"I'm game," Les answered.

But even as the two old friends started up opposite sides of Main Street, the remaining gunman scampered away.

"He's gone," Les mumbled as he kicked brass bullet casings across the street. The Phelps's wagon had been the perfect shield.

"You know it was Ballinger," Willie said, bitterly staring at the bright lights of the saloon. Music rolled through the air, and shouts of defiance followed.

"One of these others'll swear to that."

"They'd have to be crazy to do that, Les. They'd never live to see a trial. And Ballinger's done no murder. Worst that can happen is you'll lock him up awhile."

"Attempted murder can bring twenty years in Kansas."

"Your witnesses still might get their heads blown off by Ballinger before the trial."

"So what would you do?"

"Should've done it already. But I suppose you haven't got my options."

"You're right. I swore to uphold the law."

"I didn't. My only aim is to see Ellen through this."

"And the law?"

"What law? Your law? Macpherson's law? They're not the same things, you know. You mean well enough, Les, but if you play this game by your rules, you'll wind up shot in the back. Macpherson can't have all the odds on his side. That's why I won't wear your badge. He won't know for sure what I'm up to. That'll unsettle him."

"Seems to me it'll only make him more determined to settle scores with you first."

"Good. Let him try. I can take care of myself."

"There are those who can't," Les said, turning back toward the Trent house. The lanterns illuminated a scene of dismay. Ellen and the doctor huddled with the children on the porch. Two windows were blown apart. Other bullets had torn holes in the door, and one of the shutters hung loosely on its hinges. The eyes of little William and his brothers told it all. Pure terror blazed in those once innocent blue pools.

"I'll see this isn't repeated," Les promised, angrily staring at the groggy prisoners Ty was herding toward the house. "I promise, Ellen, Jack, they'll pay for what they've done."

"Maybe," Willie said, shaking with exhaustion. "That won't stop Ballinger, though. Macpherson knows he's short on time. He's got to do something soon or fold his hand. The trail herds are crossing the Nations. It's bound to turn serious."

"Wouldn't you say it already has?" Trent asked.

"No," Willie said, frowning as he shook his head. "This little show was for Les and me. They meant to draw us out, catch us off-guard. If they decide they want you, Doc, they'll set your roof afire, toss in a keg of black powder, blow you to smithereens. It's a long way from being as bad as it'll get."

"Lord, help us," Ellen said, rocking baby Anne nervously as she gazed up the street.

"Praying's a good idea," Willie said, flashing a weary smile at her. "Meanwhile, we'll see if we can't unsettle Macpherson a bit, eh, Les?"

"Sure," Les agreed, grinning.

CHAPTER 10

Any hope that Lester Cobb's two prisoners might prove of use in countering Rufus Macpherson's plans was laid to rest when a pair of pistol shots shattered the peace around 2:00 A.M. Ty Green rushed into the street, crying out for help. Willie managed to pull on his pants and run downstairs in time to learn that someone had silenced the prisoners forever.

"Had to be somebody they knew," Les said as he pointed to the bodies. Both men lay beside the rear window of the cell. A single bullet had been fired at close range into each of the bushwhackers' heads.

"So I guess you've got your three bodies after all," Ty told Willie.

"It's not the same thing," Willie grumbled. "Not at all. This way it's Macpherson who's sent the message: 'You work for me, best not be caught.' Some may leave him over this, but those who stay will stick till the end."

"He's right," Les said glumly. "What's more, there are other windows about. Ty, you bolt the door at night from here on out. I wish Ellie could send the little ones off someplace. It's too far to Texas, and we've got no family hereabouts."

88

"Yeah," Willie said, sighing. "Looks like the ante's been boosted."

Les nodded, and Ty kicked a rock at the back of the jail.

The shootings at the jail and the attempted ambush at the Trent house stirred even the most silent citizens of Edwards to action. By noon a meeting of the town council had been held. Angry storekeepers and farmers demanded new action. There was no elaborate vote or expensive campaign this time. A thunderous shout approved desperate measures. By late afternoon Ty was tacking notices up all over town.

NOTICE

THE TOWN COUNCIL OF EDWARDS, IN ORDER TO PRESERVE THE PEACE, HAS ENACTED THE FOLLOWING ORDINANCES:

1. THERE WILL BE NO CARRYING OF FIREARMS WITHIN THE TOWN PROPER EXCEPT WHERE AUTHORIZED BY THE SHERIFF.
2. ALL GAMBLING IS RESTRICTED TO DAYLIGHT HOURS.
3. THERE WILL BE NO SELLING OF SPIRITS FROM DUSK UNTIL NOON.

BY ORDER OF THE TOWN COUNCIL. A. C. WHEATON, CHM.

"You sure you can enforce that?" Willie asked Les.

"I guess we'll see. I aim to try."

"Seems like you're painting a pretty fair-sized target on that Texas backbone of yours," Wheaton said as he joined the two old friends.

"I am?" Les asked. "It's not my name on all those fool

posters. Willie, I'd move out of that hotel. It's not apt to be fireproof much longer."

"Can't burn down the hotel," Wheaton objected. "Where'd his buyers stay? Three of 'em's already reserved a room."

Ty and Les laughed. Willie frowned. Clearly time was growing short for Rufe Macpherson, and the red-haired Scot didn't seem the type to be put off easily when his goal was in sight. Where would Ballinger strike next? Willie wondered.

He didn't have long to wait for the answer. The very next morning young Rush Whitman rode into town on the bare back of the draft mule, his face and tattered shirt blackened with smoke.

"Mr. Fletcher!" the boy cried, flaying the air with his hands. "Mr. Fletcher! Help!"

Willie was sitting in the lobby of the hotel, putting a final coat of lacquer on his shelves. He set aside his brush, buckled on his Colt, and methodically made his way to the door.

"Calm down there, Rush," Les pleaded. "What's it all about?"

"Mr. Fletcher," Rush gasped, falling off the mule and racing to Willie's side, "you've got to come quick. Roy sent me. The barn's afire. Pa's got the Winchester down at the coop. He's doing what he can, but there's three of 'em."

"They burn your barn?" Ty asked, arriving out of breath after a brisk dash from the jailhouse. "Macpherson?"

"I never saw 'em, but we know just the same," Rush said, staring with hatred past the mercantile toward the cattle pens. "You coming, Mr. Fletcher? I got to get back."

"Not on that mule," Willie said, pulling the boy back from the panting animal. "He's spent, that one. What do you say to riding behind me on Thunder? He's up to a good run today, I'll bet."

"So am I," Rush said, rubbing his reddened eyes. "But we got to hurry. They could burn the house next."

"Let's go then," Willie said, turning Rush toward the livery.

"I'll be riding with you," Les announced as he followed along. "Mind the town, Ty. Maybe we can snag Ballinger."

"No, he's too clever by half to get himself trapped," Willie said, spitting at the sandy ground. "Now let's get our horses and get on along!"

The Whitman place was less than two miles from town. By the time Willie passed the stockyards, he could see the angry black smoke cloud that scarred the clear Kansas horizon.

"The barn's nigh gone, I'll bet," Rush grumbled as Willie nudged Thunder into a gallop. "Whole summer's work, that barn was, and all our extra corn gone!"

"Don't you worry about that," Willie said, searching the distant hillsides for signs of trouble. "Barns can get rebuilt. Corn grows cheap."

"You don't understand," Rush said, tightening his grip on Willie's belt as Thunder raced along.

No, I do understand, Willie thought as he spotted the simple plank farmhouse and its accompanying outbuildings. The barn was pretty well consumed, and the flames were already threatening to spread to the surrounding grass.

"They're here!" young Roy Whitman exclaimed as Willie rode past the house. Rush dropped from Thunder's side and plunged into his brother's eager arms. Mrs. Whitman cried in relief. Miles Whitman continued to exchange fire with a pair of concealed riflemen.

"Soak some blankets, get that grass dampened," Whitman called. "If that dry grass catches a spark, half the countryside will burn."

Willie nodded, then headed for the well. Mrs. Whitman tossed the boys an armload of blankets, and Les began lowering a bucket down the well's narrow shaft. Soon the boys were soaking blankets. Willie meanwhile took a spade and began digging a trench around the blazing barn.

"A whole summer's work . . . gone," Rush mumbled as he began damping out embers flying from the flaming roof.

"Oh?" Roy asked. "What would you know of it? You were still wettin' yourself when Pa and I built that barn."

"I was not!" Rush yelled.

The boys might have come to blows had not their father's sharp voice brought them back to the task at hand. A plume of dust on the nearby hillside marked the departure of the gunmen, and Miles Whitman soon joined the desperate fight to contain the flames.

Willie had never cared much for fire. He'd once seen a sea of buffalo grass aflame after lightning struck the open range. It had been horrifying. Deer and rabbits had raced in panic. Buffalo had rumbled off cliffs into the deep canyon carved by the Brazos. What had old Yellow Shirt and his Comanches called it? Sky's anger? Sometimes it certainly seemed so.

Willie watched sadly as Whitman and his boys slapped their blankets against the singed spears of grass. Les had shed his shirt and was near as black as night from smoke and ash. Willie himself was lathered and spent. The trench widened slowly. Viola Whitman strained to fill buckets and dampen blankets. After half an hour of the backbreaking labor, Willie was near exhaustion. And the task was far from finished.

"They did a fair job of it," Whitman said finally as the center beams collapsed. The barn folded into itself like a fallen house of cards. Timbers shattered, and planks snapped like twigs. The wind grew still, and the flames began devouring themselves. The surrounding grass was charred and damp. With the roof gone, there was no longer much threat of the flames spreading.

"At least we got the seeds planted," Roy said, dropping to his knees.

"Not the west twenty acres," Whitman complained. "We'll be short come winter unless the price's up."

Willie sighed and sank into the grass. He fought to keep his hands from trembling. He hadn't worked up such a sweat in weeks, and his body ached from head to toe. Rush rolled onto the ground a foot or so away. Only Les Cobb continued working.

Mrs. Whitman soon appeared with a bucket of water. Willie drank from a dipper, then splashed some of the refreshing liquid across his face and shoulders.

"I don't see how we'll make out, with no barn and all," the woman said sorrowfully. "Lucky they didn't set the house alight as well. Wouldn't have taken them more than an extra minute."

"There's time for that yet," Roy said bitterly. "Pa, what if they come back?"

"We'll hold 'em off as best we can," Whitman answered, wiping his forehead with his sleeve. "It's all there is to do."

"How can a man like Macpherson get away with this?" Roy asked angrily. "Well, Sheriff? If I was a little older, I'd walk right up to Macpherson and shoot him dead. That's how you'd do it, isn't it, Mr. Fletcher?"

"That's not the law," Les objected.

"Law?" Roy asked, shaking his head. "What law? Mr. Fletcher, how much would it take to pay you to shoot Rufe Macpherson? I'll bet we could raise the cash among the farmers alone."

"I don't shoot men for pay," Willie declared.

"I heard different," Roy said, nervously gazing into Willie's angry eyes. "There's talk you fought with the cattlemen down in the Cimarron country. They say you shot your share of farmers."

"Did they?"

"I heard Zac Waller saying you were younger then, still fresh from the war," Rush broke in. "He said you're all used up now, worn and rattled."

"And what do you say, Roy, Rush?"

"It's not for them to say one way or t'other," Whitman said, trying to shield Rush from Willie's livid gaze.

"Roy? Rush?" Willie asked. "Spell it out. Come on!"

"I think they're afraid of you," Roy said soberly. "I saw Ballinger that first time. He's worried."

"But not *too* worried," Willie said, laughing to himself as he sprawled out on the ground. The sun sent down a soothing warmth from above. A gentle breeze stirred the leaves of the nearby trees. Willie closed his eyes and drifted away.

"It's time I got back to town," Les announced an hour later. "You coming, Wil?"

"You'd be welcome to stay the night, Mr. Fletcher," Mrs. Whitman offered. "We could get you a hot bath."

"There's plenty of coals to heat the water," Roy said, laughing as he pointed to the embers of the destroyed barn.

"It's best I go on back with the sheriff," Willie explained. "I never finished the shelves back at the hotel."

"Thanks for the help," Whitman said, shaking each of the two men's hands in turn. "If ever I can . . ."

"Watch yourself," Willie cautioned. "You could wind up with a deputy's badge."

Willie winced as he saw Viola Whitman's face lose its color. The boys seemed equally concerned.

"I've got a deputy," Les reminded them all. "Let's get along back to Edwards and see what mischief he's gotten himself into."

The trail back to Edwards was clearly cut through the tall grasses. Willie and Les ignored it and swung wide eastward, then came in from the back streets. Willie took the horses to the livery while Les headed down Main Street to the jailhouse. All seemed perfectly quiet. Then . . .

Willie froze in his steps as a shotgun blast tore through the twilight air. He dropped Thunder's bridle and raced toward the stable door. By that time two rifle shots split the air. He trotted up the street in time to see a shaking Ty Green stumble out of the jailhouse and collapse.

"Ty!" Willie shouted.

The young man sat up, blinking away an avalanche of pain.

"They were waiting for me," Ty explained.

"Who?" Willie asked.

"Don't know. They were behind me. Les went after them."

Willie frowned, grabbed Ty's discarded shotgun, and took up the chase. Soon he had joined Les Cobb. The twosome slipped down a narrow side street, then slithered along a wall. Up ahead a pair of shadows merged with the gathering darkness. The flash of a sharp rowel caught Willie's attention. A second look convinced him. One of the shadows was wearing Mexican spurs.

"You take the left," Les instructed. "I'm going right."

"Hold up," Willie warned. "It doesn't feel right to me."

"You saw Ty," Les said, his anger taking charge. "They won't face me. They've got to burn farmers' barns and club youngsters barely out of grammar school."

"Les!"

"Take the left," the sheriff said, and Willie reluctantly nodded. Soon they wove their way down the shrouded street. For a moment all seemed to go well. Then a rifle shot flashed out from behind them. Les spun around, then collapsed as a second bullet shattered his kneecap.

95

"No!" Willie shouted, diving to the ground as the gunmen ahead fired shotguns. Willie dropped the first one, then chased after the other as he fled toward the stockyards. The rifleman behind them had vanished without a trace.

"I'll see you pay for this, Macpherson!" Willie called out defiantly as he started back toward Les. "Twice over!"

Les lay in the dust, bleeding from his wounds. Aside from the knee, the first shot had torn into the sheriff's side above the hip. Willie stuffed a bandana into the hole, then lifted Les and carried the sheriff back to the jailhouse.

"He's not . . ." Ty began as Willie moved past the wounded deputy.

"Get Doc Trent," Willie instructed. "Now!"

Ty didn't argue. Instead the young man stumbled down the street. A short time later the doctor arrived.

"This is where I take charge," Trent said, easing Willie away and taking over. "Leave it to me, Wil. I know my craft well."

"Sure," Willie said, sighing.

"One thing first," Les grumbled, fending off Trent's hands. "Willie?"

"You better let the doc tend you," Willie argued. "There'll be time for other things later on."

"Willie?"

"Go on."

"Wire Mackay. See to it . . ."

"I know what to do. I'll send the message. You just rest up."

CHAPTER 11

Willie was up half the night fretting over the fate of Lester Cobb. The sheriff bled himself white, and twice he howled out in agony so that the haunting echo of his voice seemed to ring throughout western Kansas. By morning the demons that plagued the wounded lawman gave up, and Les dozed peacefully in a bed sat the Trent house.

Willie waited on a narrow bench on the Trents' porch for word on Les's health. Beside him sat a restless Ty Green. Ty's head was heavily bandaged, and his bloodshot eyes were filled with a mixture of pain and anger.

"Did you send the wire?" the young deputy asked.

Willie nodded.

"I suppose until MacKay gets here, I'm in charge."

Willie nodded a bit more reluctantly. Ty stroked the barrel of a shotgun that rested against the wall. Willie felt the icy touch of his Colt. He wanted to warn Ty, explain that it wasn't for a mere boy to tackle the likes of Reed Ballinger. No, it's not for me to say that, Willie thought. A man comes of age as life demands, not as nature intends. He'd learned that at Shiloh the rainy morning when he'd killed for the first time at sixteen. It seemed as though he'd been fighting ever since.

Even so, Willie thought to warn other young men against taking that path. It was a road that, once taken, rarely offered its traveler another route. Every rock, every hill and valley, turn and fork, spoke of death and dying.

"You know there's talk about that Ballinger's been given free rein," Ty finally mumbled. "I can't take 'em all on, Wil. Nobody else'll do a thing, not now that Sheriff Cobb's been shot."

"I know," Willie confessed. "Best to keep an eye open from here out."

"The mill's sold out to Macpherson. The Hawkins farm and the Delsey place are gone as well."

"The smart ones. They can see where things are headed."

"What're you saying? That I should go, too? You think I could leave town with my tail between my legs like Walt Hummel? I'm not made that way, Wil."

"Shame. It'd be healthier for you. Can't say I criticize you for it, though. I was never much good at backing off myself."

"The two of us could finish Macpherson."

"And what would that prove? That the law was right?"

Ty hung his head, and Willie sighed.

"I guess I'm on my own then," Ty whispered.

"We all are," Willie lamented.

By the time Les Cobb was out of danger, the town of Edwards was a changed place. Three out of every four shops bore Macpherson's name, and those that remained mattered little. Each day more wagons made the long, solemn ride down Main Street, taking families east or west or north toward a different future. No throngs of citizens gathered now to curse Rufus Macpherson. Gangs down at the stockyards readied the pens for Texas longhorns. Chicago buyers moved into the hotel.

He's won, Willie told himself as he paid his daily call on the Trents. Strange that it could be so easy. Old Mike

Dunstan had said it back on the Cimarron, though. Go for the top man. Take him, and the others fall into line. Les had been that man.

I should have shot Reed Ballinger that first day in the street, Willie told himself. Or when he tormented the Whitmans. No one would have found fault with the act, not even Ellen. But then he'd been too weary of the killing. And yet as he looked down that hazy road that led into the future, he knew what awaited him.

"Mr. Fletcher!" a voice called then, startling him back to the present. Willie turned in time to see a frantic Rush Whitman flying down the street. The boy collapsed against Willie's shoulder.

"What's wrong?" Willie asked. "Your folks have trouble again?"

"N-no, s-sir," the boy stammered between pants. "It's, well, it's only that we're l-leaving. I d-didn't have much chance to th-hank . . ."

"Slow down," Willie urged, clamping a hand on the boy's shoulder and steering him to a nearby bench. "Who's leaving? What's happened?"

"Pa's sold the place," Rush explained. "Didn't have much choice. Corn burns, too. Soon it'll be too late to get a crop in elsewhere. There's good land up in the Dakotas. Pa got word from the Brocks. We'll be up there in a week or so maybe."

"It'll be better for you," Willie said, forcing a smile onto his face. He'd never thought the Whitmans would run.

"Pa would've stayed," Rush said solemnly. "Roy wanted to. But they would've come again. This time they'd've finished the job. There's Ma to consider. And I know Pa worried about me."

"He needn't have, eh?" Willie asked. "You could take on Ballinger's bunch single-handed, I'll bet."

"Yeah," the boy said, rising to his feet. "Just wanted

you to know. It's not 'cause we're cowards. Some'll say so, but they won't be right."

"You look after your family, Rush. Remember me to them."

"Oh, they'll remember. Good-bye, Mr. Fletcher."

"*Vaya con Dios,* Rush," Willie said. "We used to say it down in Texas. Go with God."

"You'd best keep Him with you for a time. You're apt to need Him more'n we will."

Willie nodded, then frowned as the twelve-year-old scampered off down the street.

Worse news soon arrived. No sooner had Willie passed the jailhouse than a spindly legged telegraph boy greeted him with a message.

"From Hays," the boy declared.

"Word of MacKay?" Ty Green asked, joining Willie.

Willie unfolded the message and read it carefully.

WILL COME STOP EXPECT DELAY STOP MACKAY

"Bad news?" Ty asked.

"MacKay's held up. We may be on our own for a while yet."

"If he doesn't come soon, it'll be a wasted effort," Ty grumbled. "More people leave every day. Won't be a town soon. Just Macpherson."

Willie handed the wide-eyed youngster two bits, then turned up the street. It was best Les know.

"I was worried Thom might have trouble getting away," Les responded to the telegraph. "Guess you and Ty'll have to hold on till I'm better."

"You won't be walking on that knee for several weeks yet," Willie said, staring at the bindings that held Les's leg in place. "Lucky you haven't lost it. Trent's a fair field

100

surgeon. Wish we'd had him in the Wilderness. I lost two good men to butchers that day."

"Ellie says the people are leaving," Les said.

"Even the Whitmans."

"Figures. Macpherson wants that land along the Arkansas for grazing."

"Could be we've drawn a losing hand this time around, Les. Maybe you ought to talk to Trent about leaving."

"Why don't you?" Les asked. "You're the expert where leaving's concerned."

"Sure I am. I'm still alive, though."

"You've collected enough holes in yourself over the years. Willie, sooner or later a man's got to find himself a place and stick. Running here and there's no good."

"Neither is getting buried."

Willie left his old friend alone and made his way outside. For a moment he stood alone on the porch, watching the exodus from town. Then he felt a soft hand grasp his wrist.

"What is it makes him stay, Willie?" Ellen asked, nodding toward the front door.

"Les?"

"No, Jack. Why can't he go as the others are doing? Or stay and doctor cowboys and stockmen. There'd be more money in it."

"Can't say for sure," he said, pulling her closer. "A sense of rightness maybe. It's bound to get him killed, Ellie. The townsfolk are leaving. It's time. Load the kids in a wagon and pull out. No one here'll blame you for it."

"I waited for someone once," she said sadly. "You. First all those hard years when you were growing tall off in Virginia. Then later after you came home. Don't you think I should stand by Jack?"

"I don't care two bits for him. It's you I worry about, you and the little ones."

"You hardly know them."

"They might've been mine, though. I guess it's as close as I'll ever get to having a family of my own. I'd have you safe, and them besides."

"And you think maybe we're in danger here?"

"You are. There's no maybe to it. The same fellows who shot Les could set their sights on you."

"Then you're in even worse danger, you and Ty."

"I can see trouble coming, Ellie. I'm on familiar ground, so to speak. But a five-year-old doesn't know about shotguns and coal oil."

"You won't let it come to that, will you?"

"I'm not enough to stop it. I did Les little good."

"He's not dead. He says if you hadn't been around, they would have challenged him in the streets. Not even Ballinger's sure he can take you on."

"He'll have help."

"Then maybe you're the one who should leave, Willie. I couldn't stand to lose you again."

"Lose me? You don't even know me."

"Don't I?" she asked, clutching his wrists.

"No," he said, a chill suddenly settling inside him. "I'm not sure you'd care to."

"You're wrong," she told him.

"Maybe, Ellie," he said as he wriggled free of her grip and started down the steps. "Wouldn't be the first time."

The walk down Main Street wasn't a pleasant one. Macpherson's lackeys were busy pulling down signs and hanging banners. TILLET'S DRY GOODS became MACPHERSON'S GUN SHOP. MRS. HOGAN'S PARLOR became MAC'S SILVER DOLLAR SALOON. Ballinger had Tarpley and Waller at work, too, tearing down the new posters announcing Jack Trent's ordinances.

"So much for our town," Wheaton told Willie back at the hotel. "Macpherson's named himself mayor. We've never had one before, just a council. In another week you won't recognize this place."

"Sure I will. It'll be Abilene and Wichita and Dodge City. It'll be the Cimarron all over again. There'll be death and dying for nightly entertainment."

"It's got to be stopped!"

"How? Even if Thom MacKay and a dozen deputies rode in here, Macpherson would only hire more men, kill more people. A few more fires would start. A kid or two might vanish. Maybe the ladies' prayer meeting would get shot up. Don't forget, I've seen how it works. Macpherson's nobody's fool."

"Maybe it's time somebody took out Macpherson. 'An eye for an eye,' as the Good Book says."

"That might work, but wouldn't it just prove we're no better than he is?"

"We'd know different."

"But would we *be* different?"

Willie thought for a time about giving up, surrendering to what now seemed inevitable. But the vision of Ballinger's laughing face taunting Ellen and the children sent shivers down Willie's spine. He decided to try another tack.

Willie wove his way through a tangle of scrawny children outside what had been Nolan's Bakery. Al Nolan was giving away what scraps of bread and pies, rolls and biscuits Ballinger's men hadn't scattered to the winds during a noontime raid.

"I've sold the place," the baker explained to anyone who'd listen. "This belongs to Macpherson. Enjoy! What I leave for him should choke him."

Willie smiled grimly at the thought, then crossed the street and made his way up the stairs and inside the church. He discovered Reverend Henshaw praying at the altar.

"Reverend?" Willie asked.

"Mr. Fletcher, if you'd be so kind as to remove your hat," the minister said after glancing up briefly. "I'll be with you shortly."

"Sure," Willie agreed, taking a seat on the front bench and setting his hat down beside him. The minister continued praying, then sat across the aisle and wiped his perspiring forehead with a handkerchief.

"What brings you into God's house, Mr. Fletcher?" Reverend Henshaw finally asked. "We don't see you often."

"I never found much religion inside walls," Willie explained. "What I've known of God's been out in the country. But that's not why I came. You know what's happening outside?"

"The town's disintegrating. People are scattering to the four winds."

"You have to do something. A man like you, somebody who's looked up to, can take a stand, rally the people."

"To what? I speak my mind, but it's not my place to set one man against another."

"Isn't that what you were doing during the vote?"

"I was only supporting Jack Trent's views."

"I'd say it went beyond that. You said once how Macpherson was an evil. Have you changed your mind about him now that he owns most of the town?"

"Don't insult me, Fletcher. You've no right to point a finger at anyone. You walk in here with a pistol on your hip. You're no better than Macpherson yourself. I know you knew Ellen Trent once. Everyone's seen the way you gaze at her. No, sir, don't you point fingers."

"I don't," Willie said, frowning. "I see you do it pretty well, though. If I've made mistakes in my life, and I have, nobody's suffered more for them than me. As for Ellen, I'll never be the cause of her coming to harm. Now, back to Macpherson. You won't speak out?"

"Fletcher, evil's always with us in one form or another.

104

It's up to good people to do what they can. My preaching wouldn't stop Rufe Macpherson, but it might get our church burned. What would that accomplish?"

Willie stood up and walked halfway to the door. He stopped and turned, then bit his lip. He wanted to accuse the reverend of self-interest, of taking the coward's way out. But wasn't the preacher doing the very thing Willie'd advised Ty Green to do? Didn't a minister have a right to look after his own hide?

"I guess your business will improve some, too," Willie said as he continued on toward the door. "More burials, for one thing. More sin means more guilt. Yes, there'll be need for preaching."

CHAPTER 12

Edwards was a quiet town no longer. Those citizens not fleeing north or west were totally cowed. Some even welcomed the air of lawlessness that came with Macpherson's rule. Town council meetings were a sham. Macpherson or Reed Ballinger would make a motion, then gaze about the room with eyes that warned the others not to object. When Jack Trent rose to speak, he was loudly jeered and often escorted from the hall.

"Why don't the people speak up?" Trent asked Willie. "Don't they care?"

"I suppose they care," Willie said somberly. "It's just they've seen the high cost of standing in Macpherson's way. What's more, some will profit from the trail herds. The cafes will see business like never before, and even the laundry'll have a turn of good fortune. Places like Wheaton's hotel will top a year's receipts in a single fortnight."

"You think I'm wrong to fight on?"

"I never said that," Willie told the doctor. "I'm a poor man to tell anybody when to give up. Shoot, I've fought my share of lost battles. I rode in Southern gray till Appomattox. I've been with the plains tribes hunting buffalo. I never handed over my sword, not once."

"But you think we're finished here in Edwards."

"No man's through who doesn't want to be," Willie said with blazing eyes. "Doc, the truth is I admire men who stick to their guns."

"Me included?"

"You especially. You've got the kind of life I always figured to have."

"With Ellen, you mean?"

"And the kids. You've got a place to call home, the respect of your neighbors. Me, I'm just another relic left from the war, a drifter who never settles long in any one place."

"You're not so old that you can't change."

"Old?" Willie asked, laughing to himself. "Not in years, I suppose. But I've got too many notches carved in me. There's little peace in my future."

"You could go somewhere far away, make a fresh start."

"Where?" Willie asked, his eyes reddening slightly. "The Rockies? Dakotas? I've been there. Nothing ever really changes. Life's gentle and quiet for a time. Sooner or later someone comes along who pushes a little too hard, and I take my stand. The killing follows pretty quick after that."

"And you think it'll happen again here?"

"Don't you? You're bound to've talked to Ellie. She knows. Les does, too."

"Knows what?"

"That if you don't give it up, sooner or later Reed Ballinger will set his sights on you. That's when I'll kill him."

Willie turned away. He couldn't see the doctor's expression. He wondered if Trent marked his words down to bravado. After all, how could anyone else know the hardness,

107

the stone-cold grip that seized Willie's heart before he drew that Colt?

As for Ballinger, the gunman had exchanged his dusty chaps and buckskin vest for a broad-brimmed black hat and a tailored suit. The Colt was ever in evidence. So was the six-pointed silver star he wore just above his heart.

"Thought we ought to have a sheriff fit to make rounds," Macpherson announced. "Cobb's not recovered from his wounds, and young Ty's hardly up to the task."

"No?" Ty asked, storming out into the street. "Try me."

"It'd be my pleasure," Ballinger replied coldly as he tore the last of the ordinance posters from the jailhouse wall. "Go ahead, boy, call your tune."

Willie rushed out beside young Ty and gripped the young man by the shoulder.

"Let go!" Ty demanded, shaking loose. "I'm not some scared farm boy who's come running for help. I'm the law, what's left of it anyway."

"No, I'm the law!" Ballinger taunted, rubbing the badge with his fingers. "You're just a boy who used to be a deputy here. Right, boss?"

Macpherson nodded, and several of the stockmen who'd gathered laughed loudly.

"Turn over the badge, Ty," Mrs. Henshaw urged. "Don't let them kill you, too."

"They haven't yet," Ty grumbled. "He thinks he's fast. Let's see for ourselves."

"No," Willie pleaded. "He doesn't think. He knows. This isn't the time or the place."

"And just what is?" Ty implored. "When the whole town's turned into a saloon? When all the people have moved off? Have you seen who's moved into the Whitman place? Thirty girls from the Colorado goldfields. Pa would have stood up to them."

"So his boy'll do it for him, eh?" Ballinger asked, stepping out into the street and making a half turn so that the sun blazed down over his left shoulder.

"Ty, please," Willie said softly. "I'll need you."

Ty gazed up into Wil Fletcher's solemn eyes and frowned.

"Here," the young man cried, plucking the deputy's badge from his shirt and flinging it toward Ballinger. "Take it. You'll never be the law here, though. Your day'll come!"

Willie wondered if that was so. Two days later the first of the trail herds arrived, and Main Street filled with bands of free-wheeling Texans. When not paying a visit to the Whitman farmhouse for a bit of companionship, the cowboys roamed the shops and stores of Edwards, drinking and brawling and firing pistols in the air. Whiskey and greenbacks were exchanged as if there were no tomorrow. Music filled the streets long after darkness fell upon the land, and many a night was disturbed by the sounds of shattered glass and splintered wood.

"This must stop!" Jack Trent declared after a pair of cowboys paraded down Main Street, bashing in every window they passed. Even though the drovers made good the damage, the doctor sent Ty Green to Ft. Dodge with a plea for help from the army. Soon thereafter a silver-haired captain arrived with a squad of soldiers to investigate.

"Welcome to Edwards, Captain Stroud," Macpherson boomed out from the Silver Dollar Saloon. "Come along in. Have a drink. Your men, too. The Army never buys its own liquor in my town."

"Well, Rufe, that's most kind," the captain said, grinning. "Sergeant, why don't you and the boys refresh yourselves while Mr. Macpherson and I have a walk around."

Willie frowned as the two men set off toward the stockyards.

"Macpherson's even bought the army," Ty grumbled.

Captain Stroud expressed it differently.

"Look, Dr. Trent," the soldier said when the doctor greeted him. "I can't interfere with civilian authority. Most folks seem plenty happy with things the way they are. If things are a little noisy, well, there are towns in Kansas that would welcome a few greenbacks."

"And if our children can't sleep?" Trent asked. "If our wives can't walk Main Street without being accosted by a dozen drunken cowboys?"

"Keep 'em at home," the captain advised. "Come September, the cowboys'll be gone. The little ones can get all the sleep they want then."

Trent turned away in disgust. Worse, a wire arrived from Thom Mackay saying his arrival was still weeks away.

"What's to be done?" Trent asked in frustration.

"Wait and hope for a change," Willie answered.

Change was often a long time coming, though. And as the pens filled with nervous longhorns, everyone in town seemed to be prospering. Wheaton never had an empty room, and Jack Trent stayed busy patching up cowboys and townspeople who blundered into their way.

Wil Fletcher occupied himself completing the last of Wheaton's cabinets. Another carpenter might have hurried the work to a conclusion weeks before, but Wheaton was in no great rush to lose Willie's labor, and Willie welcomed the excuse to remain in Edwards. When the last of the lacquer was stroked on the wood and the final knob was screwed in place, Willie turned his attention to the gaming tables Wheaton had set up in the lobby. Most mornings those tables filled with cattle buyers and trail bosses, all eager to try their luck at filling an inside straight or collecting three queens.

Willie sat in on a game now and then. He listened as the conversation turned to Texas and cattle. A storm of mem-

110

ory engulfed him as one or another of the cattlemen spoke of the wild hills and ravines of the Brazos country.

"You sound a bit Texas to me yourself, Fletcher," a San Antonio rancher named Collingwood commented. "You ever call Texas home?"

"I've been most places at one time or another," Willie said.

"But you know Texas," Collingwood said, nodding to himself. "The state has a way of marking men. I see it in your eyes when anyone talks about the Brazos."

"It was once home," Willie confessed, "but not since before the war."

"Served in the army, did you?" a buyer named Crawford asked. "Cavalry, I'll bet."

"Toward the end. When we weren't eating our horses, that is."

The others joined in a round of laughter, then continued with the game.

"I find you a puzzle, Fletcher," Collingwood said after Willie had bluffed his way to a pot on a pair of sevens. "I can usually size up a man by the way he plays his cards. You, though, jump around like a jackrabbit. One minute you're bold. The next you turn cautious. What's a man to make of you?"

"Oh, he might guess I'm not all I seem," Willie told them.

"Any fool could see that," Collingwood continued. "No carpenter I ever saw played cards so close to his chest. And I don't think you carry that Colt to hammer nails with, either."

"Not all you seem?" Crawford grumbled. "That mean you're more or less?"

"One or the other," Willie said, grinning.

"Well, my friend, puzzle or not, you'd best keep an eye on Reed Ballinger. I've seen him at work before. He makes

111

short work of those he puts on his list. I see him watching you. You're bound to be right up there on top of that list."

Willie nodded. It was likely true. But he didn't let the thought slow the game any. Betting was as fast and furious as ever. And the pots grew and grew.

He was holding three tens when a pistol shot tore through the hotel's side window and splintered the new shelves inside the room. The poker players scattered, and Willie raced for the doorway. Outside a pair of drunken cowboys were firing pistols. Their fire was returned, and one fell bleeding in the dusty street. The second dropped his gun and stared ashen-faced at his fallen companion.

"You had no call to shoot him, Reed!" the surviving drover cried. "You shot him dead."

"You fools could've killed somebody innocent!" Mrs. Henshaw shouted from the church.

"They nearly did!" Emma Franklin screamed.

Only then did Willie notice the Franklin woman cradling a bundle on her knee.

"Lord, help me!" the cowboy exclaimed as he raced toward the woman. Little Zelda Franklin, all seventy pounds of her, was bleeding from a shattered leg. Her younger brother Aaron clung to his mother's skirts and sobbed.

"We're sorry, ma'am," the cowboy said. "I'll make good on this. I've got some money, and . . ."

"You think you can buy your way out of this trouble?" Mrs. Franklin cried. "My little girl's nigh crippled. You might have shot us all."

"I promise you, ma'am, I'll pay for a doctor. We'll get the leg mended right."

"I'll see it's not repeated," Ballinger said smugly. "These boys just get a bit carried away. You understand."

Mrs. Franklin would have none of it, though. She gazed first at the line of cowboys across the street, then stared at her neighbors.

"How long will we allow this to go on?" she called. "What does it take to open your eyes? Does one of us have to die?"

The crowd stirred, but Ballinger motioned for Waller and Tarpley to break it up, and those with no business on the street sought shelter.

"It'll be a long time before the people forget what's happened today," Ty said angrily. "If you joined with me, we could end this now."

"There are too many of them," Willie warned. "Be patient, Ty."

But even as he spoke the words, Willie knew they wouldn't be obeyed. Youngsters were never long on patience, and Willie was far from the perfect man to be giving that particular advice.

CHAPTER 13

Willie sat on the steps to the porch of Ellen's house, sadly gazing down the street at a pair of rowdy cowboys wrestling outside the mercantile. Across the way three boys returned from afternoon errands. Willie couldn't ignore the fear that filled the youngsters' eyes. It was only a matter of time before pistols again disturbed the peace of the Kansas afternoon, before other bullets struck out at the innocent.

Young Zelda had escaped with a shattered leg. Even now the girl lay on a feather bed in Ellen's bedroom, trying to understand how fate could be so cruel as to condemn her to a life of lameness.

"How do you explain to an eight-year-old that she'll be crippled the rest of her days?" Ellen had asked a half hour before. "How many more have to get shot before somebody does something? Who will it be next? We're running out of beds, Willie!"

Yes, he thought as he listened to the shouts drifting down the street from the saloons. Les was healing slowly. Others had left. And each time Willie looked into Trent's eyes, he could tell the doctor was ready to speak out, to make a stand.

"Still here?" Trent asked from the door.

"Thought I might talk to Les a bit," Willie said, sliding over as Jack Trent joined him on the steps.

"Something's got to be done, Fletcher. It could be William next time. Or Ellen."

"It's not the time," Willie warned. "Ballinger's eyes and ears are good as ever."

"Meaning?"

"You speak out again, and you'll be as good as dead. Look across the street there."

The doctor followed Willie's pointing finger to where Zac Waller sat. Waller's Colt revolver hung loosely on his right hip, ready should the opportunity present itself.

"I can't just stand by and watch—"

"They'll kill you," Willie interrupted. "Quick and sure. You'll be little use to anybody that way."

"I'm no gunfighter, Fletcher. I won't go facing off in the street with them."

"No, you'll use that fine way you have with words on 'em, won't you? You'll never hear their answer. It will come from the midnight shadows, two barrels of buckshot and a round of drinks."

Trent stared sorrowfully at Waller, then turned his head toward the house.

"You know I'm right," Willie went on. "You'll do them no good dead."

And so Jackson Trent held his tongue. More trail crews arrived. The stockyards filled with longhorns, and the saloons overflowed with drinking, free-wheeling Texas cowboys. Violence spread down Main Street. Daily it seemed some cowboy fired on another, while Ballinger busied himself less with dispensing justice than with settling accounts at the saloons or the mercantile.

"It's got to stop," Ellen cried the day she and several other mothers carted up the schoolbooks and moved the school to the Arnaud farm on the north side of town. "We're all of us dying."

Willie bit his lip and glared at Reed Ballinger. The gunman stalked the street like a mountain lion, ready—no, eager to pounce on his prey. His shiny badge turned Ty Green more sour by the day. Willie preferred to avoid Ballinger, to keep cautiously to the shadows.

One afternoon, however, even Willie was unable to ignore the noise. A band of Texans marched down Main Street, shooting pistols and tossing rocks. In a quarter hour they shattered half the windows in town. Cowboys shot the tails off weathercocks, peppered flour barrels, tore shutters off houses, and terrorized those few townspeople venturesome enough to step outside.

"Not the church!" Reverend Henshaw pleaded as the drovers aimed at the simple oak steeple atop the roof. "Spare God's house!"

"God's house?" one of the cowboys asked, laughing loudly. "Why, everybody knows God lives on the cattle trails. He don't abide these stinkin' Kansas farm towns any better than we do!"

"That's enough!" Ty Green shouted, emerging from behind a water barrel back of the old schoolhouse. "You've no call talkin' to the reverend like that."

"Go home to your mama, boy!" Ballinger shouted, stepping out to block Ty's path.

"Out of my way, Ballinger," Ty said, shoving the sheriff.

"Now, that wasn't altogether smart, boy," Ballinger declared as he threw Ty down into the dusty street. "Attackin' the sheriff! I'll see you locked up for that!"

"You may wear that badge, but you're not the law," Ty said for what seemed the hundredth time as he glanced around at the gathering crowd. "You don't know the meanin' of justice. You let these drunken fools threaten good people like the reverend, shoot down little girls and harmless farmers. Well, it's time all that was settled."

"And who'd do the settlin', huh, boy?" Tarpley asked, joining Ballinger in the center of the street. "Huh, boy?"

The crowd laughed heartily, and Ty opened his coat so that a pair of matching Colts could be seen.

"You?" Ballinger cried. "You?"

Willie by now had joined the throng. "No!" he called. "Ty, no!"

"It's time somebody stood up to them!" Ty answered, turning not only toward Willie but to the assembled townspeople. "This is our town. They've got no right to take it away from us. If you won't do anything, then I will!"

"Ty, wait!" Willie called.

"Leave him be," Zac Waller urged as he blocked Willie's path. "It's time Reed dealt with that pup."

Willie turned away, then wheeled around and struck Waller's face with an elbow. The gunman stumbled and fell. Willie slipped past and charged out into the street.

"Make your move, boy," Ballinger growled at Ty.

"He's young," Willie argued as he stepped toward Ballinger and Tarpley. "Let it pass, Ballinger."

"I'm the law here now!" Ballinger shouted, rubbing the badge as if the resulting gleam might lend him more authority.

"You came by that badge in the dead of night," Ty said hatefully. "Stole it like a coyote takes his dinner. Long before you ever got here, I swore an oath."

"Stop it, Ty," Mrs. Henshaw pleaded. "They'll only kill you."

Willie started to speak again, but the feeling of cold steel in his back froze him in silence. Waller had recovered enough to pull a pistol. Tarpley moved over to block Willie's approach.

So, here we are again, Willie thought as he gazed nervously at the two gunmen, then past them to where Ty Green squared off with Reed Ballinger. A vision of a dozen young cavalrymen charging through a field west of Five Forks appeared in Willie's mind. Willie himself had been what, nineteen, twenty? A long volley of Yank carbines had torn the ragged gray line to pieces. How eagerly those boys had charged to their deaths!

Willie had watched it all from a hundred yards away, pinned to the earth by a disabled mount. He'd been helpless, even as he was now. Ty faced Ballinger bravely, stood his ground like one of those knights Willie and Ellen had once read of in his mother's storybooks. But this was no story, and there were no happy endings ahead. Ty drew a pistol, and Ballinger did likewise. Age and experience blended with cold-blooded accuracy. Before Ty could aim, Ballinger fired. The bullet struck the former deputy in the right thigh. Ty spun around. His Colt fell harmlessly to the ground.

"Ballinger!" Willie shouted. Tarpley and Waller moved nearer.

"So, you'd shoot a sheriff, would you, boy?" Ballinger asked, leveling his pistol as Ty stared up with terror-filled yes. Ballinger fired again, and the bullet slammed into Ty's chest. The youngster fell backward.

"Get out of my way," Willie growled, slipping away from Waller and pushing Tarpley aside as he rushed toward Ty's fallen body. He knelt beside Ty as the young man coughed out his life.

"I . . . I tried," Ty stammered.

"I know," Willie said, holding the young man's head. Ty shuddered, then gazed skyward.

"It's so blue, Wil, so blue."

"Yes," Willie agreed as Ty coughed again, violently. Blood trickled from the young man's mouth, and his breathing grew labored. Then the eyes froze, and Willie knew that death had again paid a call.

Yes, Ty, you tried, Willie spoke silently to his fallen friend. And now you're dead.

"You all saw it!" Waller called out as an angry crowd assembled. "That boy called Reed out, challenged the sheriff. Wasn't anything else Reed could do."

"It was no better than murder," Reverend Henshaw declared. "Pure murder."

"No, it was a fair fight," Rufe Macpherson announced.

"Fair?" Willie asked, angrily turning toward Ballinger. "Fair? He was only a boy."

"Old enough to carry a Colt," Tarpley said, laughing. "Old enough to get himself killed."

"As old as he's apt to be," Ballinger added.

"Think it's funny, do you?" Willie asked. His eyes widened, and his lip quivered with ill-concealed fury. "Care to try your luck again . . . with me?"

"Reed?" Waller asked, quickly joining Ballinger. Tarpley stepped more cautiously away, and the crowd scattered.

"There are three of us," Ballinger said sternly. The smile had vanished.

"There are now," Willie said coldly. "Won't be in a minute or two."

"Reed?" Waller asked, his fingers trembling slightly as he read the icy confidence in Wil Fletcher's eyes.

"Not today," Ballinger finally answered. "There's been enough bloodshed."

"The wrong blood," Willie declared. "I tell you this for a fact, Ballinger. You harm anybody else in this town, I'll be coming for you. You may not see me, but you'll know. And you'll think the devil himself's after you."

Macpherson clapped loudly and shouted from the opposite side of the street. Willie turned instantly in that direction. Just as quickly the smile fell from Macpherson's face.

"I've got words for you, too," Willie said, stepping backward so that he could keep one eye on Ballinger. "I don't promise you'll be the first or the last, Macpherson, but I'll see you worked in there somewhere. This is your handiwork, and it's written in scripture. Reap as you sow!"

CHAPTER 14

The townspeople of Edwards gathered again the following morning to lay to rest young Tyler Green. Reverend Henshaw spoke glowingly of the young man's courage, but as daybreak spread over the Kansas plain, all Willie could think of was the price paid for the momentary mistakes of youth.

"He was doing my job," Les Cobb complained when Willie related the news of the shooting.

"No, he was taking up for all of us," Ellen objected. "It's like when Willie and Trav signed the muster book and went off to fight the Yankees. The others all had reasons for staying home. Some had families. Some had fears." She turned and smiled at Willie. "It's not so different here. You were foolish to go, Willie, and I was angry at you. But I suppose I was proud, too."

"Of Ty as well, I suppose," Willie mumbled.

"Yes," she said, staring out the window.

She spoke on about the idealism of youth. Willie heard little of it. He was too burdened by the memories of other deaths and other times. He felt cold inside, and his fingers tapped the wall nervously.

"You shouldn't blame yourself, either," Ellen whispered

to him. "Les didn't ask you down here to get yourself shot. There were too many of them."

"So now there's one less of us."

"Yes," she said sadly.

Ty's death had a profound effect on the townspeople. Even those who'd previously voiced no opposition to Rufe Macpherson seemed outraged at young Ty's shooting. Jack Trent put it simply.

"We're none of us safe now," the doctor told a gathering at the church that night. "So long as Reed Ballinger walks Main Street, we're all in danger. He'll use that badge as a license to kill. Who's to be next? You? Me? Our wives and children?"

"No!" the crowd cried.

"If only the army would have done something," Sarah Henshaw lamented. "Or if Marshal Cobb hadn't been shot."

"Maybe one of us should ride to Dodge," Wheaton said, rising slowly and gazing at his neighbors. "We could hire a man."

"No," Trent objected. "We can't stoop to Macpherson's level. Whatever we do, it has to be legal."

"Like Ty's murder?" Wheaton asked.

The crowd grumbled, and Trent motioned for silence.

"We'll draft a new charter," Trent suggested. "We'll hold fresh elections."

"And what of Macpherson?" Wheaton asked. "Look, Jack, we'd like to do it your way, but while you're campaigning, what do you suppose Reed Ballinger will be doing?"

"We'll convince even Macpherson that we'll have a better town without all this shooting."

"Convince?" Wheaton asked, shaking his head. The others murmured disagreement.

"Reverend Henshaw will help, won't you?" Trent

asked. "The ladies can speak to their husbands." The crowd grew louder. Small quarrels erupted between friends and neighbors.

"Enough!" Willie finally shouted. "Jack, you mean well, but this is pure lunacy. You can't fight Reed Ballinger with words. We tried that. It's what got Les shot!"

"Yes," the others agreed.

"Laws are just pieces of paper," Wheaton declared. "We have to find a way to answer Macpherson's guns."

"Ty tried that," Willie reminded the innkeeper.

"One boy can't do it," Trent said somberly. "It will take all of us."

"Doc, most of us are married men," farmer Arnaud said. "We've got wives and children to consider."

"That's just why we have to act," Trent told them.

"He's right!" Mrs. Franklin shouted. "Each time I look at little Zelda, I wonder why the people of this town let something happen like that. A poor child can't walk safely home from school. Now it happens to young Ty Green. Are we people or animals? We've got to do something."

"Yes!" the crowd responded.

As the men gathered around Jackson Trent, Willie stepped outside.

"They're forming a citizens' committee," A. C. Wheaton said as he joined Willie outside the church.

"They've had a town council," Willie grumbled.

"They never carried shotguns. The men on this committee will."

"It could work. I've seen towns rise like this before. Just depends on how much backbone they have."

"There's strength in numbers."

"And if Macpherson's boys start shooting?"

"Some'll stand. I will. We're meeting at first light. I'd like to think you'll be there. We can use you."

"I've never been much of a joiner."

"You served in the army, or so I'm told."

123

"Even then I did my best work scouting the enemy, raiding supplies with my company. I wish Thom MacKay was here. Men are going to die before the week's out, and I'd sure feel better if a man who knew what he was doing was having a hand in the planning."

"You could be that man."

"You don't know me," Willie mumbled.

"I know this much. It was you who walked out in the street after Ty was shot. Ballinger's backed down twice, and both times you were out there. I saw his eyes. He was afraid. You weren't."

"Neither was Ty. I've seen cowards live to see their great-grandchildren."

"We'll need you tomorrow, Wil."

"I'll be around, but it's not my play."

"That may change."

Willie nodded, then gazed sadly down the street to where the lights blazed brightly in the saloons. Music drifted through the air, and voices joined in song.

At first light Jack Trent collected his citizens' committee on the steps of the town hall. Others congregated nearby. A. C. Wheaton nailed a proclamation to the front door. There were a lot of words, but boiled down it simply meant the people of Edwards were taking their town back.

"What's all this?" Reed Ballinger shouted, stepping out into the street and rubbing the slumber from his eyes. He'd not taken the time to slip on a shirt, but his gun belt was securely fastened around his waist.

"You're through, Ballinger!" Mrs. Franklin shouted. "You and your kind aren't welcome here anymore."

"Quiet, old lady," Ballinger growled as he started across the street. "You bunch of fools! Clear out. You're in my way!"

"Are we now?" Wheaton asked, turning the first of five shotguns on the gunman. "We plan to stay in your way."

Ballinger paused a minute. Glancing into the faces of the committeemen, he smiled.

"Zac, where are you?" Ballinger yelled. "Ben?"

Waller and Tarpley came stumbling out of a saloon. They stopped halfway across the street.

"What in . . . ?" Waller asked.

"I'd shed those pistols, boys," Trent said, stepping out from the others. "It's against the law in Edwards to carry sidearms."

"I *am* the law in Edwards," Ballinger declared. "You men are all under arrest."

"Who's going to lock us up, Ballinger?" Wheaton asked, raising the barrel of his shotgun. "You? We take it into our heads, you'll find yourself spread over half the county."

"Zac, you go gather some men," Ballinger ordered.

"Hold up there," Wheaton said, swinging the shotgun in Waller's direction. "You're going nowhere till you shed that pistol."

"Don't go pushing your luck, Wheaton," Waller said with angry eyes. "You'll find yourself dead before you fire that scattergun."

"No, he won't," Willie announced, taking a deep breath before approaching Waller and Tarpley. Willie couldn't help smiling as he walked. This time the extra guns were on his side, and Waller and Tarpley knew it.

"We won't be forgettin' this soon, Fletcher," Tarpley said as Willie removed the gunmen's pistols from their holsters.

"You look over there," Willie said, grinning as he pointed to the shotguns. "Remember that. They could just as easily have shot you this morning. Kindhearted, these shopkeepers."

"They'll likely be remembered that way by their widows," Ballinger declared.

Willie started toward Ballinger, but the commotion had

125

attracted attention by now. A herd of drovers spilled out of the saloons and boardinghouses. A crew stormed down Main Street from the stockyards. Leading the way were a pair of scarlet-dressed harlots from the bawdy house outside of town.

"Never knew they got up this early," Wheaton said, laughing.

"Brazen hussies," Mrs. Franklin declared. "How dare they!"

"Maybe we should disarm them, too," someone suggested.

The men laughed loudly, but they grew serious quickly enough. Two dozen or so drovers joined with ten stockmen in the center of Main Street. Each carried either a rifle or a pistol. Ballinger spread them out in a line. Willie retreated a dozen steps and readied himself for the confrontation.

"So, you mean to call the tune, do you, Trent?" Ballinger asked. "You ready to die?"

"You ready for war?" Willie yelled back. "We're not talking about a pistol or two here. Death will rain like a Brazos thunderstorm if you force the issue."

Ballinger grinned, but the words had an effect on the drovers. Trent and his companions stood their ground, though one or two nervously tapped the ground with their toes.

"Hold on there a minute," a tall stranger called from the hotel. "I can't afford to bury half my outfit."

Willie turned and examined a familiar face. The man wore the new suit and shiny boots of a trail boss just returned from the tailor. His forehead was etched with the wrinkles left by some thirty-five years of fighting Comanches and Yankees and Texas winters.

"That you, Major?" the trail boss asked Willie.

The voice struck a chord. Willie studied the face, the movements.

126

"Slocum?" he finally asked.

"Heard you were dead, Major," Slocum said, marching with outstretched hands toward Willie.

"Hold up there," Wheaton warned.

"It's all right," Willie said as he gripped his old comrade's hands. "We fought together in Virginia."

"And a time or two thereafter," Slocum said, waving his men out of the street. "We've got no quarrel here, boys. Go get yourself a drink and leave Macpherson to settle his own problems."

"We don't need those Texans!" Ballinger yelled. "There aren't but ten of these fool storekeepers!"

As if in answer, shutters parted from upstairs windows. Winchester barrels appeared from behind wagons and water troughs.

"Half the town's armed!" Waller cried in disbelief.

"I guess it's not our day," Ballinger said, laughing loudly. "Let's go have ourselves a drink with the drovers, boys. There'll be time to settle this score another day."

Willie watched Macpherson's crew retreat silently to the saloons.

"What about their guns?" Mrs. Franklin asked.

For an instant Trent seemed ready to challenge the stockmen, but Willie flashed a warning.

"Little point to it anyway," Wheaton declared. "Macpherson can find guns easier than he can find men. He doesn't seem to be short of either."

"No," Willie agreed, shaking his head.

"So, shall we have a drink and refight a few battles?" Slocum asked.

"I've spent close to ten years trying to forget," Willie answered.

"Then maybe we ought to discuss the future."

"Sure," Willie agreed, following his old companion toward the hotel.

127

Tension remained high those next few days. Jackson Trent had his Citizens' Committee walking the street in pairs all day long. Others kept watch from upstairs windows. Macpherson's men ruled by night, and the saloons and gambling parlors continued to do a land-office business. The hospitality tents along the Arkansas and the fancier farmhouses outside of town housed most of the drovers.

"Nothing's really changed," Trent grumbled. "Ballinger still walks out there wearing a sheriff's badge, and they laugh at our decrees."

"Nobody's been shot," Willie told the doctor. "That's some comfort. Most of the drovers are leaving their pistols with their saddles, and if the drinking's as steady as before, at least the fighting's dying down."

"For how long, though?"

"Who can say?" Willie asked, shrugging his shoulders. "Be thankful for each hour, each day. Herds don't reach the railheads much after July, and the late ones might prefer Dodge anyway."

"Maybe you could ride out and talk to some of the ranchers. They might not come here if you argued against it."

"Me? I've not been on the trail from Texas in years. Money does the talking, and Macpherson's got his buyers all lined up in a row, just waiting to toss Yankee greenbacks at these herds."

"Then maybe the cowboys would go on to Dodge once the herds are sold."

"Some already have. I suppose I could speak on that. But in truth, it won't solve your problem."

"And what would that be?"

"Rufe Macpherson. He owns this town, like it or not, and he's got the men to settle this issue if he decides to. You watch yourself, Jack. The night has eyes."

Trent nodded, and Willie headed toward the hotel. Once there, he joined a heated card game. As he spoke with buyers and trail bosses, he argued against staying in Edwards.

"I rather like it here," one buyer replied. "Dodge City is too rowdy by half. Here Rufe takes care that we're kept contented, and the steers roll along in."

"Most of my boys side with Macpherson," Slocum told Willie that night when they shared a roasted chicken in the cafe down the street. "They don't take to shotgun-wavin' farmers walkin' the street. It's like you're sayin' our money's fine to take, but we're not welcome to hang around. A Texan feels a bit bare without his Colt. You know that. We don't trust these Kansas Yankees much."

"There are other places to spend your dollars," Willie pointed out.

"If it came down to it, which side might you line up with?" Slocum asked.

"I've pledged myself to help Dr. Trent," Willie said soberly. "You know me, Ted. You rode with me across half the country, from Appomattox Court House all the way back home to Texas. In all that time I never went back on my word, did I?"

"Seems to me you've gone astray a bit, though, Major. I never would've figured you livin' out your years in a Kansas hotel, lookin' after the interests of shopkeepers and chicken raisers. There're still fortunes to be made in Texas. Me, I used my first wages from the trail to buy land, roped a few mavericks, and now I've got five thousand acres on the Clear Fork of the Brazos."

"Do you ever run across Trav Cobb?"

"Do I? He's out to Sunday supper once a month."

"Trent's married to his sister. Trav's brother Les got himself shot here a few weeks back."

"Sister?" Slocum asked, scratching his head. "I never recall but one sister, that one bein' the sweet yellow-haired

129

gal that you spoke of every night since you joined up with us in Richmond. You were bound to marry that one, Major."

"Should have. But things fell apart back home, and I drifted away from her. She did better for herself."

"Did she? Well, I never knew you to give up a thing you really wanted."

"I've given up more than you know."

"The boys say you built yourself quite a reputation down on the Cimarron. Now it appears' you're choosin' sides again. It's a fair way to get yourself killed."

"I've gotten through worse times."

"You got me through 'em, too, Major. Back in Virginia you were a fair man in a fight. Lord knows I was glad enough to find myself elbow-to-elbow with a scrapper. I'd as soon stay to the same side as you. All my boys want here is a bit of liquor and some entertainment. Dodge isn't but a few hours away. I'll suggest they head in that direction. I'll speak to some of the others, too."

"I appreciate that."

"I could lend you a good man or two. Jed Henderson's good with a rifle, and Ken Holland's fast. They'd be steady if it came down to it."

"Thanks, but I'd not see others brought to grief."

"You know Ballinger won't meet you face-to-face if he can do it th'other way. I saw his handiwork back in Young County. He's cold-hearted, and he don't mind shootin' women or little ones. That Cobb girl could find herself in the middle of this."

"I've urged her to leave, but she was never short of spirit, Ted. The children are too young to make the trip to Trav's place, too."

"I wish you well with it," Slocum said, shaking Willie's hand. "If you get through this and need a place to lay low, you'd be welcome at the Diamond S. That's what I call the place. It's twenty miles upriver from old Fort Griffin. An old Brazos raider like yourself should have no trouble findin' his way there."

"Thanks," Willie said, "but I can't see myself going back. The Trident ranch isn't home anymore. It's not mine."

"And here?"

"That's the trouble, I guess. No place is really home. I got lost back in '66, and I can't seem to find my way."

"Texas never really leaves your heart, Major. It's a fair place for beginnings."

"It was once. But now..."

"Still is. Why not try your hand at ranchin'. I'd loan you enough to get started. Trav and I could give you some stock."

"Thanks," Willie said, grinning as he glimpsed it in his mind. But Ellen's shining face broke through the vision, and he shook his head. "I've got work here, though. Maybe, when it's all over, I'll head down that way, pay you a call."

"You'd be welcome. The boys'd love to see you. I got myself five of them, you know. Second one's called Will for you."

"I'm honored you thought of me," Willie said, forcing a smile onto his face. "But if you knew what I've become, you'd choose another name. Seems like I pick a new one for myself each time I move on."

"More's the pity, Major. But you always did know best what to do. I'll be leavin' in the mornin', headin' home. I could use some company."

"*Vaya con Dios*. Let Him be your companion."

"Better he stay with you, Major. You're apt to be more in need of Him just now."

Willie frowned. Hadn't young Rush Whitman said pretty much the same thing?

    *   *   *

"Watch the trail, Ted," Willie called out when Slocum headed south the next morning. And as the rancher passed from view, Willie couldn't help thinking the trail south was far easier than the one Wil Fletcher would walk in the days to come.

CHAPTER 15

The uneasy peace lasted less than a week. New trail crews arrived in Edwards, and not all the drovers were eager to surrender their arms.

"You can't call this a cattle town!" they complained. "We'd feel more welcome in a wolf's den."

When two outfits swerved around Edwards and drove their herds along to Dodge City, Rufe Macpherson made a rare visit to the hotel.

"You're killing this town," Macpherson told A.C. Wheaton. "Those longhorns passing us by are our life's blood. It's cowboys and my stockmen who buy the goods, eat the food, rent the rooms in Edwards. Without us, the whole place will dry up and blow away."

"The town was here before you came," Wheaton reminded Macpherson. "It'll be here when you're gone."

"I'm going nowhere," Macpherson insisted. Then, seeing Willie, he added, "You have feelings for that doc and his family, Fletcher. You speak with 'em. I've got no taste for blood. But if it comes down to it, we'll do what we have to."

"Now you listen to me," Willie said sourly. "I told you

before. You bring harm to Jackson Trent, you'd best be prepared for the consequences."

"You're all of you fools!" Macpherson said, shaking his head as he departed. "Fools!"

"A.C.'s worried," Jackson Trent said to Willie after Wheaton had passed on Macpherson's warning.

"Aren't you?" Willie asked. "The last time you pressed him, Les got ambushed. Watch yourself."

"You, too," the doctor said. "I've seen them watching you. Tarpley or Waller, one's always sitting across the street, keeping watch."

Willie nodded, but he knew it was Ballinger who merited concern. When a crowd of angry stockmen gathered on the steps of the church a hair after noon, Reed Ballinger was in the middle of them.

"I expected something like this," Wheaton told Willie as they joined Trent and Walter Galway, the barber, outside.

"Was bound to happen," Willie said as other shopkeepers emerged from their stores. Each carried a shotgun.

"So what now?" Trent asked.

"See those two cowboys in front of the mercantile?" Willie asked. "Get a man over behind them. Send a couple to the hotel. Get them on the roof. Be ready."

Trent issued instructions, and men took their positions. Others watched behind rifles pointed out of upstairs windows and from atop rooftops.

"Well, boys, it's time we showed these shopkeepers and pig farmers a thing or two!" Ballinger shouted as he waved the stockmen into the street. Waller and Tarpley followed. The others stared at the rifles and shotguns that lined their pathway.

"Reed?" Waller asked.

"You're not afraid of them, are you?" Ballinger asked his companions. "Come on. You'll see. They'll lose their nerve."

"Will we?" Willie asked, stepping in front of Jack Trent. "It's a lot to ask a man to die, Ballinger. Especially for a stockman's pay."

"There's twenty dollars in it for each one of you!" Macpherson called from the safety of the town hall.

"That'll hardly buy a headstone," Wheaton declared, laughing. "You'll need one, boys!"

The stockmen retreated a few steps. They exchanged worried looks, and Ballinger stomped his foot angrily.

"What're you waitin' for?" the gunman bellowed. "Come on!"

Ballinger stormed on down the street, but a rifle fired from the roof, kicking up a spiral of dust a foot from Ballinger's toe. Ballinger froze, and the stockmen scattered in a dozen different directions. Even Waller and Tarpley sought shelter.

"This isn't finished!" Ballinger yelled. "Bet on that!"

"It's finished today," Walt Galway declared. "Go get yourself another drink, Ballinger. Maybe you should find yourself some land."

The shotgun-wielding citizens of Edwards laughed heartily, and Ballinger glared at them. For a minute Willie thought there might be an exchange of gunfire, but Ballinger slowly turned and withdrew.

That night A. C. Wheaton set up two long tables in the hotel ballroom, and food was brought over from the cafe down the street. The leading citizens of Edwards gathered to celebrate their victory over Ballinger's mob. Jackson Trent and A. C. Wheaton made brave speeches. Willie sat at the far end of the table flanked by Ellen's young sons William and Cobb on one side and by a pair of farmers on the other.

It reminded Willie of a wedding feast. Platters of beef and mounds of potatoes were passed along the table, and he wondered if there was so much as a pinch of flour left in town. He smiled as he watched Ellen feed the little ones. In the flashing eyes of young William, Willie saw something of the Ellen he'd left behind. He couldn't help feeling haunted by the closeness, by the laughter Jackson Trent shared with his family.

That might have been me, he thought, dropping his chin into his hands. Where did it all go wrong?

"You don't seem to be enjoying yourself much," Wheaton said to Willie. "Not still worried about Macpherson, are you?"

"I've got a lot on my mind," Willie answered.

"Ease up, Wil," Trent urged. "We've beaten them."

"I learned a long time ago that winning a skirmish doesn't end a war. At Shiloh we chased the Yanks almost into the Tennessee River. The next day they drove us all the way back to Corinth. Macpherson's not about to call it quits. He won't let a few shopkeepers alter his plans—not for long. If you were smart, you'd make a deal with him, drive a bargain while you still can. As it is, he's bound to turn on you like a crazed bull and hit you hard. You've got him boxed in a corner. He'll fight like fury."

Willie swallowed before continuing. The glitter faded from Ellen's eyes, and he was sorry he'd spoken. "It's what I'd do," he told them. "It's how the game is played."

"We're not down on the Cimarron," Walt Galway said. "It's different here."

"Is it?" Willie asked. "Wait and see."

The words chilled the room. Wheaton and Trent seemed particularly unnerved, and Willie himself gazed with wild eyes at the distant street. Darkness had settled over Edwards. It was Macpherson's town now.

That notion weighed heavily on Willie's mind. Perhaps that was why he insisted on escorting Ellen home. They led the way, she carrying tiny Anne and Willie gently leading Ellis and Cobb by the hand. William trotted alongside, babbling away in his high voice about summer stars and longhorn cattle.

"See, you needn't have worried yourself," Ellen declared when they arrived at the Trent house. The streets appeared deserted, and not even a chirping cricket disturbed the silent night.

"I'll always worry," he told her as he released little Cobb and rested three-year-old Ellis on one shoulder. "An old habit, I suppose."

"Would you help put the boys to bed?" she asked. "Might call for a story or two, but as I recall, you never ran out of them for Jamie."

An image of the younger brother left behind in Texas flashed through Willie's mind. It brought a smile to his face, and the boys instantly jumped at the idea.

"As soon as you've got your nightshirts on and settle down," their mother said, nodding to Willie. "Now get along inside, boys."

William led his two brothers to the storeroom that had been converted into a bedroom following Les's shooting. Ellen took the baby to the back room where a crib stood opposite the small bed still occupied by poor, lame little Zelda Franklin. Willie paused to share a moment or two with Les before William appeared in an oversized nightshirt.

"I see you're getting acquainted," Les said as William dragged Willie toward the open door.

"So it'd seem," Willie said, shrugging his shoulders.

Willie sat on the edge of the small bed shared by the three youngsters. They huddled around him, eager to hear the tale spun by the well-traveled stranger. Ellen watched from the doorway, her golden hair shining in the glow of a single candle.

"Once, a long time ago, the world belonged to the buffalo," Willie began. Before he could say another word, gunshots shattered the silence. The front window exploded in a hundred pieces, and a man's voice cried out in pain.

"Oh, God!" Ellen cried, extinguishing her candle and rushing toward the boys. Baby Anne let out a shriek, and young Ellis clung to the bedpost.

"Papa!" William called, climbing out of the bed.

"You stay here and look after your mama," Willie told the boy. "See she stays inside." Then, turning to Ellen, he said, "Keep them low, Ellie. I'll see to Les."

"I've got to get the baby," she said, rushing past him out the door. The boys started to follow, but Willie blocked their path.

"No, it's for me to do," he said solemnly as he drew out his pistol. "Get down and stay put. No matter what."

The boys nodded, and he read in their fearful eyes the all too familiar signs of terror. Willie wasn't really surprised. It was bound to come to this.

He made his way slowly, cautiously down the hall. He found Les kneeling beside a window, holding a Winchester rifle.

"They're across the street," Les said, motioning for Willie to stay clear of the window. "Ellie all right?"

"She's looking after the baby," Willie explained.

"You'd best see to the others."

"Others?"

"On the porch," Les explained. "Jack, Wheaton, another one, too, I think."

Willie nodded, then slipped back down the hall and raced to the front door. A pair of sharpshooters continued to fire at the house. Les answered them from the front bedroom. The porch was strangely, ominously silent. Willie cracked open the door, then shrank back as bullets splintered the hinges and left the door hanging strangely ajar.

A figure raced across the street toward the house. Willie

dove through the open door, aimed, and fired. The charging gunman spun in a circle, then fell.

"Best get to cover," Wheaton said as he dragged a wounded Jackson Trent toward the safety of the door.

"What happened?" Willie asked as he shielded the groaning doctor.

"We were out here talking—Jack, Walt Galway, and myself. They must have been waiting across the street."

"You just stood here in the open?" Willie asked as the riflemen resumed firing.

"I suppose we were fools, but how could we know?"

Willie shook his head and helped drag Jackson Trent on inside the house. The doctor bled freely from a bullet wound in the leg. Willie ripped open Trent's trousers and examined the wound.

"Don't mind that," Trent said, groaning, as he tore a strip of cloth from his shirttails. "I'm the doctor, remember?"

"I'll see it's bound," Wheaton promised.

"I'll get Galway." Willie started for the door.

"He's dead," Wheaton said as he began binding Trent's leg. "Guess I'm the lucky one."

Willie frowned as Wheaton revealed the tear in his arm caused by a rifle bullet.

"Let me . . ."

"You'd best see to the ones across the street," Wheaton said, pointing toward the door. Willie nodded, then crawled outside and huddled behind Galway's corpse. As his eyes adjusted to the darkness, he detected three shadows lurking behind a wagon fifty feet away. Another hid behind a water barrel.

So, Willie thought as he took a deep breath. It's started all over again.

The figure at the barrel stepped out and fired at the house. Willie aimed his Colt and fired. The shot struck the figure in the left boot heel, and the man cried out in pain.

The three at the wagon fired in Willie's direction, but Les opened up with the Winchester, and soon all three crept off down the street. The one by the barrel limped after them. Willie paused a moment, then ran across the street and dove to the ground just short of the barrel.

"Come on!" one of the bushwhackers cried out. "They're after us!"

Willie started to rise and fire, but his attention was drawn by a shiny piece of metal inches from his right hand. It was the rowel of a Mexican spur.

"Well," Willie mumbled, fingering the broken rowel. "The darkness hasn't hidden everything."

By now the fleeing gunmen were halfway to the other end of Edwards. Willie let them go. He turned back to the Trent house, pausing only long enough to gaze at the shattered body in the street. He turned the corpse with his foot. It was one of Macpherson's stockmen, a thin man named Whitaker.

Willie bothered no further with Whitaker, though. He trotted on to the house, passed Galway's bloody corpse, and made his way inside. Les Cobb stood in the parlor holding a Winchester.

"They get away?" the former sheriff asked.

"All but one. I may have nicked another."

"I'll watch the front. Wheaton's guarding the back. You might see if you can help Ellen tend Jack."

Willie nodded, then stumbled through the broken glass and shattered furniture to Trent's infirmary. The doctor lay on the table. Ellen dabbed iodine around the wound.

"Looks like you get to be the patient this time, Doc," Willie said as he joined her.

"Ever take out a bullet?" Trent asked.

"More than a few," Willie admitted.

"Care to try now?" the doctor asked.

"Now wait just a minute, Jack Trent!" Ellen fumed. "I've been your nurse now seven years. You weren't the

140

only one in Wichita. Don't you think I know what's to be done?"

"Ellie," Willie objected.

"Don't you start with me, Willie. I've cut more things out of your hide than you'd care to admit. Now step aside and give me some light."

Willie moved out of the way, and Ellen took charge. After setting out the proper instruments, she dabbed a cloth with chloroform and held it to her husband's face. Trent coughed, then grew quiet as the chloroform took effect.

"Hold the leg still while I cut," Ellen instructed. Willie gripped Trent's leg and held it still while Ellen cut. She probed for the bullet, then skillfully drew it out.

"You did that well," Willie remarked as she ran an instrument under the flame and prepared to cauterize the wound.

"Does it surprise you?"

"Everything about you surprises me," Willie answered, grinning at her. "Always has."

"And I thought we knew each other inside out."

"Maybe we did . . . once. That was a long time ago, and we've each made a new world for ourselves."

She tried to force a smile in answer, but the night had brought on a weariness. She bandaged Trent's torn leg, and Willie helped her carry the unconscious doctor down the hall to his bed.

"Is Papa hurt bad?" little William asked as Willie stepped back into the hall. "You won't let him die, will you?"

"No," Willie told the boy. "Your mama's taken good care of him. He'll need your help getting around for a time, but he'll be just fine."

"Till they come again," Wheaton said.

"That won't happen," Willie declared, snatching the rifle from the innkeeper's hands.

"Fletcher?"

"You won't need this for a while," Willie explained. "I've got some hunting to do."

As Willie filled the rifle's magazine and reloaded his Colt, Les did his best to argue against the ill-advised action. It wasn't till Ellen joined them in the parlor that Willie paused, though.

"I've seen that look before," she told him. "Wait for Les to get well. MacKay should be here soon."

"There's been enough waiting," Willie declared, pointing to three bullet holes in the wall beside him.

"There's been enough dying, too," she said.

"It could've been worse, Ellie. What if little Anne or William had been out there? What if they'd come through the back?"

"Stop it!" she begged. "Isn't it enough that Jack's lying in there with a hole in his leg? You told me yourself. At night this town belongs to Macpherson."

"I've got to do something!" he shouted. "I can't just stand by and watch . . ."

"Tomorrow," she pleaded. "Get some rest tonight. I'll fix you some breakfast, eggs fried light like you used to like them. Maybe a little ham, some potatoes sliced really thin."

Willie sighed. Her eyes blazed brighter than the candles burning on the parlor table. He'd never be able to argue with those eyes.

"I'll sleep across the door tonight. At first light I'm settling things with Macpherson. I warned him."

"We'll talk of that in the morning," she said, bending over to give him a kiss on the forehead. "Don't be in such a hurry to get yourself killed, Willie. You may think you're a loner, but there are those who still love you."

More's the pity, he thought as he watched her go. More's the pity.

CHAPTER 16

Wil Fletcher slept as promised on a pair of blankets across the threshold of the Trent house. Twice he awoke at the sound of a dog barking down the street. A third time he rose to discover a wren hopping about on the porch. The fourth time he watched a tall shadow move cautiously down the street. Willie sat up, shed the blankets, and cradled the Winchester. The stranger discarded his horse's reins and continued toward the door. A pistol hung loosely from a gun belt, and he carried a shotgun as well.

"Hold still," Willie called as the dark figure stepped to the door. "I've got a rifle aimed at your forehead. Ease that shotgun down and explain yourself."

"Gladly," the man said, leaning the shotgun against the porch rail. "I've been sent for."

"MacKay," Willie mumbled, recognizing at last the voice of the federal marshal. "It's about time."

"I wired you three days ago. Got no answer."

"Likely Macpherson's boys bought off the telegrapher. Come on in, Marshal."

MacKay took the shotgun and stepped inside. Willie did his best to make a path through the parlor toward the infirmary. Wheaton had laid Walt Galway on the table, and MacKay glanced sourly at the body.

"Happened last night," Willie explained. "Dr. Trent caught a bullet in the leg, too. Wheaton, who owns the hotel, was nicked. I got one of them. The rest got clear."

"And Les?"

"He's getting better, but he's still not fit for what's needed."

"And that is?"

"Settling this," Willie said grimly.

"You mean to do it all by yourself, Wil?"

"If I have to. I told you up in Colorado I do my best work alone."

"We made a fair team that time."

"And could again."

"Any proof who did the shooting?"

"Still playing marshal, are you? Have a look at this."

Willie tossed the torn rowel to MacKay. The marshal nodded and returned it.

"You're not looking to lock these men up, are you?" he said.

"They fired bullets at me last night, MacKay. Did it before, too. The gunmen who shot Les wore Mexican spurs like the ones this rowel belongs to. They came here again in the dead of night, shot dead one man and close to killed another. There were children in this house last night."

"And a woman."

"I won't see her harmed, Marshal."

"I'll cover you if I can. If they agree to surrender, though, I'll see they come to trial."

"Reed Ballinger? He wears Mexican spurs."

"Heard he was here. The state'd be better off without him, but that's for a jury to decide, Wil."

"No, I'll decide that," Willie promised.

The two men talked a bit more before catching some

much needed sleep. Willie went back to his blankets, and MacKay dozed nearby. They were awakened at first light by a crowing cock. Soon thereafter William announced breakfast.

"You haven't lost your touch, Ellie," Willie said as he finished the first of two eggs on his plate.

"You ought to see what she does with a pot roast," Les said.

"Her true talent's still frying Brazos catfish, though," Willie said, closing his eyes a moment and remembering.

"We're a long way from the Brazos, Willie," she said. "But we pull a catfish out of the Arkansas now and then."

"Papa takes us fishing," William said, staring sadly at the empty chair the doctor should have occupied.

"He will again . . . soon," Willie said, cutting up the second egg. "All this trouble will soon be over."

"Willie?" Ellen asked.

"MacKay's here now," he told her. "It's time we settled things."

"Is it?" she asked.

"Yes," he declared, pausing to look her in the eye. "I won't ever risk another ambush, not with you and the little ones here. I should have insisted you leave the day I got here. Now all I can do is settle accounts."

She rose and walked away. Willie thought he detected a tear on her cheek. He finished his breakfast and went after her.

"Ellie?" he called.

She turned and faced him with a solemn, tear-streaked face. Her lips quivered, and she gripped his wrists with trembling fingers.

"I sent you off to battle before," she whispered.

"I came back."

"Did you?" she asked. "You changed. I've seen Reed Ballinger and his kind before. I've watched men die. Some were just boys out to prove they were men. Others were

145

like you, cold, their hearts eaten away by years of war and killing. They died just as quickly, just as . . . alone. Willie, please, let Thom MacKay do it his way."

"It's past that now," he told her. "This is personal. I've tried it their way, watched all the new laws and regulations. You can't write the greed out of a man's heart. Life is cheap out here. I've watched gentle folk burned out of their homes. I've seen children made orphans . . . or worse. Someone's got to put an end to Rufe Macpherson. I'm the one to do it. This is an old game with me, Ellie. I'm good at it."

"Willie, no."

"I can't change what's happened the last dozen years. If I could, maybe I would. But what's done is done. I've got to go."

"I'll pray for you."

"You'd best save your prayers for that man lying in his bed with a shot-up leg. He'll need them, too."

"Willie, it's on my account you're doing this. You loved me once. Even now I . . ."

"Don't, Ellie. Please. I just don't think I could bear it right now. No farewells, and no more remembering. You've got a husband, a family. You still will when this is all over. Lord knows he's a better man than I ever was."

"Willie . . ."

He turned away from her outstretched hands and made his way back to the kitchen. He took his rifle, then motioned for MacKay to follow. Once outside, they were joined by a bandaged A. C. Wheaton.

"The others are ready," Wheaton declared. "Most of the drovers headed for Dodge when they heard MacKay was here. I got a recall petition signed, too. We'll vote our way out of this mess."

"Good," MacKay said, taking the papers.

"You won't solve this with papers," Willie said for what

seemed to him to be the hundredth time. "No, they drew the line last night."

The trio got no closer than the mercantile. Rufe Macpherson greeted them there. Ballinger, Waller, and Tarpley waited across the street.

"I've got some papers for you, Rufe," Wheaton called out. "Recalls you, too, Ballinger."

"I'll take your guns, boys, pending trial," MacKay said, gazing at Ballinger in particular. "You'll surrender that badge."

"On whose authority?" Macpherson asked.

"Mine," MacKay said, opening his coat so that the U.S. Marshal's badge flashed brightly.

"U.S. Marshal?" Macpherson asked, laughing. "What do I care for all the federal marshals in Kansas? Arrest me. Lock me up. See where it gets you."

"No one's takin' this badge from me," Ballinger growled, stepping into the street.

"Oh, no?" Willie asked, joining the gunman. "Looks to me like you've got a little trouble with one of your spurs, Ballinger. Lose something?"

Ballinger glanced down at his boots. The missing rowel was all too apparent.

"MacKay?" Willie asked, taking the twisted rowel from his shirt pocket and tossing it to the marshal.

"You're under arrest for murder, Ballinger," MacKay said, motioning for Wheaton to watch Macpherson. MacKay eyed Waller and Tarpley.

"Nobody's hanging me," Ballinger declared. "You think you can take me, Marshal, go ahead and try."

"No. You're mine," Willie said, stepping closer to the gunman. "I should've killed you that first time. Then again after you shot young Ty. I almost got you last night when you bushwhacked the doc. I won't miss this time."

"You got a big reputation, don't you, Fletcher? All 'cause you did a bit of shootin' down on the Cimarron some years back. Well this is here and now. I could handle the likes of you by moonlight in midwinter."

"Then go ahead and try your hand, Ballinger. I'm waiting."

Ballinger turned a half-circle so that he had the sun over his left shoulder. Willie paid little attention. Instead he closed the distance.

"I don't mean to shake hands with you," Ballinger said, stepping back. "You're awful sure of yourself."

"I can afford to be."

"Can you now?" Ballinger asked. He coughed loudly, then put his hand over his mouth. He coughed again, then drew his pistol. Quick as lightning Willie stepped to his right, drew, and fired. The two pistols discharged a split second apart, but Ballinger's shot tore into a nearby watering trough. Willie's found its target.

Ballinger dropped to his knees and stared in disbelief at the circle of red widening on his chest.

"Reed!" Tarpley called.

"You aim to join the party?" Willie asked as Tarpley stepped into the street.

Ballinger spit blood, then tore open his collar. The gunfighter's fingers seemed powerless to do more. His eyes glazed over, and he fell face first into the dusty road.

"Waller? Tarpley?" Macpherson shouted.

The gunmen drew back, and Willie walked over to Ballinger, nudged him slightly, then turned him over. Willie leaned over and snatched the badge from the corpse.

"I'll see this is returned to Les," Willie told MacKay. "It never did belong on the likes of him."

"You'll pay for this, Fletcher!" Macpherson warned.

"Oh?" Willie asked. "You're next, Macpherson. A wise man might take his chance and leave town."

"This is a long way from over," Macpherson warned before retreating inside the mercantile. Waller and Tarpley then dragged Ballinger's lifeless body down the street to the undertaker's.

"Have him make boxes for you, too!" Wheaton called to them. "I'd hate to have to throw you into a lime pit."

The Citizens' Committee gave a cheer, but Willie turned away.

"You know what this means, don't you?" Wheaton asked.

"Yes," Willie said grimly. "It means from now on they won't fight fair. They could come at us anytime, anyplace. We won't be the only targets, either."

"You never were," Mrs. Franklin said, gripping Willie's arm firmly. "Why don't you go after the others, get it over with?"

"Death leaves a sour taste in my mouth," Willie said, breaking away from the woman. "Leave me alone."

CHAPTER 17

"This is a long way from over."

Willie heard those words over and over as he prowled Main Street. His eyes swept the town, ever on the lookout for Rufe Macpherson. But neither he nor Waller nor Tarpley could be found.

"You'll hear from them tonight," Thom MacKay warned.

Willie nodded. Yes, he thought. I'll have company then. He passed most of the afternoon alone in his upstairs room at the hotel, cleaning and reloading his Colt, readying himself for what promised to be another long and deadly night. Toward nightfall he escorted MacKay to the Trent house for dinner.

Willie paused a moment outside. The front of the house still showed the signs of battle. Bullet holes pierced planks. All that remained of the front windows were a few broken panes of glass. The quilts Ellen had nailed up to block the view from the street would scarcely stop a bullet. The bloodstained porch served as a grim reminder of how close death's shadow had walked.

Inside, the parlor was a scene from a nightmare. Furniture was torn apart, and though fragments of glass had been swept from the floor now, the evening sun cast eerie shadows across the walls.

"I wasn't sure you'd come tonight," Ellen said as she led them to the dining room.

"Couldn't think of a better place to get a meal," Willie told her. "Besides, I think Thom ought to stay with you tonight."

"And you?"

"It's better I was at the hotel."

"Better for you?"

"For you," he said, sadly touching her hand. "And others."

Ellen nodded, then stepped inside the dining room. Baby Anne and little Ellis were elsewhere. Les was seated at the far end of the table. Jackson Trent sat flanked by the older boys.

"I thank you for your help last night," Trent said as Willie took his place on the opposite side of the table. "You, too, Marshal."

"Seems I missed the party," MacKay said, nodding to Les.

"I heard what happened today," the doctor went on as Ellen carried in platters of food. "I guess you were right about Macpherson. But I was right about the law. To build a future, you have to have law."

"Not law," Willie objected. "Justice. They're not always the same."

"They should be," MacKay broke in. "It's up to us to make it so."

"That's about enough discussion," Ellen said as she set a bowl of stewed carrots on the table. "I believe it's time to return thanks for our many blessings."

They bowed their heads as she prayed. Ellen's calm, clear voice pierced Willie's heart like the jagged flint of an arrowhead. Once again he found himself remembering, and the pain was almost more than he could bear.

"Willie?" Ellen asked as she passed a platter of beef to him.

"Thanks," he said, trying to avoid the haunting sparkle in her eyes as he took the plate.

"Are you all right?"

"Just tired," he confessed.

"No surprise about that," Les remarked. "Can't stay up half the night and rise with the sun without showing a little weariness."

MacKay laughed, but Willie couldn't bring himself to enjoy the levity. He busied himself eating and left the others to talk. When plates were finally cleaned, Willie rose and silently helped Ellen clear the table.

"They'll come again tonight, won't they?" she whispered.

"That's how I'd do it."

"I'd feel better knowing you were with us."

"I'll be safer at the hotel. I can watch the street."

"Here you'd have help."

"Ever see what happens when a stick of dynamite gets thrown through a window, Ellie? You figure Les and the doc can get clear lamed up like they are? What about that little Franklin girl?"

"Her mother's taken her to the Arnauds' farm."

"And the baby? Ellis? Even William would be hard pressed to get clear. Don't you see how easy it'd be?"

"Macpherson would never do that," she declared, shaking her head. "The house would catch fire. Half the town would burn."

"You really think that would bother him much? I've seen it before. I saw a mother sift through the pine splinters looking for her babies. Ellie, trust me to know. Do it my way."

"You're only setting yourself up as a target."

"Am I?" he asked, smiling grimly. "I do my best when I'm on my own."

"That wasn't always true."

"I know," he said sadly. "But it is now."

As darkness settled in over the town of Edwards, Willie bolted the door of his hotel room and prepared himself for a long, difficult night. Downstairs Wheaton and a trio of farmers waited with shotguns. But when it came right down to it, Willie didn't expect they would much discourage Rufus Macpherson.

Willie moved a large wardrobe over to block the window, then spread a pair of blankets out alongside the wall. The loaded Colt and its companion Winchester stood ready.

So, he thought, it's now up to Macpherson.

For a time Willie drifted in and out of a light slumber. It was as close to peace as was possible anymore. For once the dreadful memories of past battles, of death and dying, released their grip. An hour after midnight he was awakened by the heavy sound of boots on the wooden stairs down the hall.

Willie sat up, flung aside the blankets, and holstered his pistol. He then huddled behind the wardrobe and readied to strike out at intruders. A shotgun might have made more of an impression, but the rifle had the edge in range.

By now Willie could hear the approach of three, maybe four, men down the upstairs hall. Someone downstairs called out, and a pair of shotguns boomed out. Pistols barked an answer. A door down the hall burst open, and a shotgun blasted the air. A voice cried out in horror. Then the bolted door of Willie's own room exploded, and a pair of gunmen burst inside. Shotguns tore the bed apart, then splintered the wardrobe. Willie rolled across the floor, then fired rapidly at the two figures standing in the doorway. The first ducked away, but the other stumbled backward, clutching his throat as he gasped for breath.

"Waller!" the fleeing gunman screamed.

Willie crawled past the dying assassin and aimed at the terrified survivor of the foiled ambush. The Winchester cracked, and the would-be killer crumpled to the floor. Two others fled noisily down the stairs, and Willie took a deep breath before following. He paused a second as he passed the splintered door of a cattle buyer.

"Poor luck," Willie mumbled as he stared at the shattered body of the buyer. Clearly Macpherson's crew had misread the room numbers.

"Fletcher, you all right up there?" a shaken Wheaton called out.

"A good deal better than some," Willie answered as he started down the hall toward the stairs. "Three up here are dead. One's that Chicago buyer."

"Lord," Wheaton said as Willie made his way down the stairs. "We're all right down here."

Willie nodded. Clearly the farmers hadn't made a very serious attempt to block the path of Macpherson's bushwhackers. Even so, a slender boy of maybe twenty stood cowering before the deadly barrel of Wheaton's shotgun.

"He come with the others?" Willie asked.

"His name's Hooks," Wheaton explained. "Stayed on after coming up the trail from Kansas. He's been helping at the livery."

"Got a better offer, eh?" Willie asked, staring hard at the young cowboy. Willie's eyes blazed furiously, and Hooks shrank back.

"Had a pair of twenty-dollar gold pieces in his pocket," Wheaton explained.

"A fair profit for a night's work," Willie grumbled. "If he'd kept to his feet a bit better."

"What are you goin' to do to me?" Hooks asked, trembling as Wheaton's shotgun grew less steady. "You can't just shoot me!"

"Isn't that what you boys did upstairs?" Willie asked. "Don't expect sympathy from us."

"I never even fired my gun, mister. I promise you. I'll ride out of here tonight. I've got a horse just outside. I promise. You'll never see me again."

"Reminds me some of young Ty Green," Wheaton said sadly. "Well, Fletcher?"

"Ty's dead. Last night it was Galway. Today that Chicagoan. And he expects mercy?"

"Please," Hooks pleaded, dropping to his knees.

"Let him go," Willie said, lifting the barrel of Wheaton's shotgun.

"What?" Wheaton asked. "He'll run to Macpherson as soon as he clears my door."

"Fine," Willie said, glaring at the young cowboy. "You go find Waller and Tarpley. Tell them they missed their chance. Now it's me who'll be coming for them."

Hooks scrambled away, and Wheaton grabbed Willie's arm.

"Not tonight!" the hotel owner argued. "Not in the dark."

"No, they'll run most of this night. But come daybreak, we'll be finishing this."

Wheaton nodded sadly, and Willie turned back toward the stairs. Oil lamps lit half the windows in town, and nervous shouts filled the air.

"They could come back," Wheaton said, staring fearfully at the door.

"Two of them won't. No, it's finished for now."

Willie shook off the anger that was building up inside him. He then stumbled back upstairs, pausing briefly to allow a pair of ranchers carrying bodies from the powder smoke-filled hall to pass by. The still faces and shattered bodies were a stark reminder of the price a man paid for his mistakes.

Willie then continued along to his room. Once inside,

he pushed the door closed, then blocked the doorway with what remained of the bed. In spite of his firm belief that Macpherson's hirelings would not return, he kept the Winchester handy as he huddled behind the wardrobe and drew the blankets around him. He knew there would be little peace that night, and even less come morning.

CHAPTER 18

Morning dawned bright and early. Willie blinked away his weariness and stared at the sunlight streaming through the partially blocked window of his room. He gazed at the door, its splintered panels a reminder of the buckshot that had shattered the stillness of the previous night. Willie slowly got to his feet, yawned, then grabbed his rifle.

Downstairs, the hotel lobby was buzzing with activity. A dozen members of Jackson Trent's Citizens' Committee gathered to plan their future actions. Willie walked past them all. He stopped only when he spotted Marshal Thom MacKay just inside the doorway.

"Well, you had company last night," the marshal said, frowning as he glanced nervously around the lobby. Buckshot peppered the walls. Tables and chairs, though righted, showed the scratches and bruises of rough treatment.

"I trust the Trents are safe," Willie said.

"I think you collected most of the attention last night, my friend. Things down on our side of town were rather quiet. You took the edge off Macpherson's boys."

"I'm glad of that," Willie said, sighing. "Now it's time to finish the job."

"That'll be easy enough. Since Ballinger got himself

shot, we've been hearing from lots of folks. We've got witnesses to last night. By noon I'll have warrants back from the district judge. We'll lock up the lot of them."

"Will you? No, you'll just give Macpherson time to get away. Or maybe he'll ride down to Dodge and hire himself another Reed Ballinger. Even if there was a trial, your witnesses wouldn't hold up. You remember how it was in Colorado. Nobody's about to testify when they know there are killers on the loose. There's only one way to settle this."

"You're wrong, Wil. There's power in a warrant."

"Power? No, they're just scraps of paper to a man like Macpherson. As for Waller and Tarpley, they're mine."

"You can't hope to take them both. I've seen you in a fight. You're good, but you're not that quick."

"Go ahead and get your warrants, Thom," Willie said, glancing out the door at the nearly deserted street. "In the end it'll come down to this," he added, tapping the barrel of his rifle. "It always does."

"Not always," MacKay objected.

"No?" Willie asked with wide eyes. "It will this time."

Willie left MacKay to make his plans. There were too many men milling about at the hotel. Outside, resting silently by the door, lay the slain. A blanket covered the face of the cattle buyer. Macpherson's henchmen were uncovered. Their terrified eyes remained wide open, seemingly as a warning of what awaited the others. Willie turned away from them and walked to the cafe. He had no sooner sat down than a frightened boy of twelve or so staggered in and fell against the table.

"Mr. Fletcher," the boy stammered.

"Yes?" Willie asked. "Do I know you?"

"I'm . . . I'm Frankie, Frankie Ross," the boy said as he gasped for breath. "My ma's the seamstress. You remember. She sews for Mrs. Trent sometimes."

Willie nodded, though in truth he didn't recall ever meeting a seamstress or this boy before.

"So?" Willie asked.

"They sent me, Mr. Fletcher," the boy continued. "Mr. Waller and that Tarpley fellow. They said to tell you . . ."

"Go on."

"They said . . . they said to tell you they're waitin' down at the pens for you."

"And?"

"And if you're not down there in ten minutes, they'll shoot my brother Donny."

Willie rose slowly and gripped the boy by the shirt.

"You got a brother, boy?"

"Yes, sir," Frankie said, quivering. "He's naught but ten. They've got Ma, too. And Mrs. Bradley, the cook over at the Fishers' cafe. They weren't jokin', Mr. Fletcher. You should've seen 'em. They'll shoot everybody, only Donny's the first."

"Run along and tell the marshal," Willie said, releasing the boy.

"I'm supposed to tell 'em what you said."

"Go tell the marshal," Willie said angrily, "and leave me to my breakfast."

The boy nodded, then raced off out of the room. Willie sipped a cup of coffee brought him by the waitress.

"Bring you some eggs?" the young woman asked.

"It appears I've got no time," Willie said, placing a half-dollar on the table. He then rose and stepped toward the door. Thom MacKay met him in the street.

"I told the boy to stay put," MacKay explained, pointing to where young Frankie sat beside Wheaton outside the hotel. "I'll bring the answer myself."

"What happened to your warrants?" Willie asked. "Give up on the law?"

"No. Just thought a friend might use some help."

"You're welcome to watch my back. Truth is, I still manage better alone."

"May be a dozen of them."

"Oh, I wouldn't guess that to be the case. More likely Macpherson's halfway to Colorado by now. This is personal."

"Men like Waller and Tarpley don't shoot a man unless it profits them. You know that. Let me get some help. We can surround the pens, take 'em easy."

"You hear what that boy said? You can only hang a man once. If they kill those others, well, it's for me to settle."

"And if they kill you instead?"

Willie gazed at the marshal and smiled. How could anyone explain what a relief that would be, how gladly some would settle for the peace that promised to follow that final breath?

"They won't," Willie finally said. "I've been here too many times. Besides, if they slipped away, they might visit Ellen next time, hold a gun to her head. Or maybe one of the little ones. I can't allow that."

"You're crazy."

"So I've been told," Willie said, grinning wickedly as he took out his pistol and checked the cylinder. "I'll tell you about it over lunch, Marshal."

"You watch yourself, hear?"

The cattle pens were at the far edge of Edwards, down by the Arkansas. A mist crept up from the river, shrouding the place so that it reminded Willie of the Tennessee ridges that morning in April back in '62 when he'd killed for the first time.

"Twelve years it's been now," he mumbled. "I've been killing men as many years as young Frankie Ross has been alive. And in all that time I've never felt quite as mired in death as I do this misty morning."

"Who's out there?" Waller called as Willie approached

the pens. "That you, boy? Come closer. I can't see you clearly."

"I left the boy in town," Willie answered, weaving his way through a small grove of willows. "I came to give my answer in person."

"That's just fine with me!" Tarpley shouted. "It's time we settled this."

"I'll settle with you," Willie declared. "You'll get the same reward I gave Reed Ballinger."

"Reed was my friend!" Tarpley cried.

"Oh?" Willie asked, laughing. "Men like us, Tarpley, we don't have friends. We ride with a man sometimes, but we don't share much save maybe a supper or two. We never know when he's apt to draw a bad hand. Or when he may hire out with the man who's sworn to kill us."

"Maybe you're right," Waller answered. "Why not come a bit closer so we can talk about it some more?"

"I'm coming," Willie promised. "Don't worry yourself over that. Now, why don't you let the others go."

"No!" Tarpley yelled. "So long as they're here, that marshal's goin' to keep his distance."

"Then it's time we got on with it," Willie said, dropping to his knees and crawling beneath the fog to where the maze of pens began. He patted a restless steer on its rump, then slipped beneath the rails of the outside fence and stepped closer to the loading platform. Beside it stood a small house. Waller and Tarpley were likely there.

"Where've you gone to, Fletcher?" Tarpley shouted. "Hang this fog!"

"No, it's bound to hang you!" Willie shouted in answer. The longhorns stirred restlessly, and he hummed softly to them. The beasts quieted, and Willie grinned. Yes, he thought, I know the ways of cattle. And men.

The sun broke through a cloud overhead, and the fog thinned out. Willie huddled behind a water trough. Up ahead Waller and Tarpley watched from the platform. A third gunman stood guard beside the door of the house. Willie lifted his Winchester and fired. The guard cried out in surprise, then collapsed. The door sprang open, and two women peered out.

"Get back in there!" Tarpley shouted.

The door slammed shut, but as Tarpley raced toward the house, Willie fired again. Tarpley dropped to the ground and crawled behind a nearby water barrel.

"He's a ghost, that one!" Waller yelled as he took cover beside the railroad tracks. "You see where he is, Ben?"

"In the pens somewhere!" Tarpley shouted. "He's got a clear shot at the house. That's certain. If he gets over there and gets atop the roof, we're finished."

"Damned fog!" Waller cursed. "Watch the north side, Ben. I've got the south."

Willie chose neither. Instead he crept like a snake through the pens, climbing rails and weaving his way through the cattle. Most of the steers had long since been loaded upon boxcars headed east. Those that remained seemed accustomed to being disturbed.

Willie finally reached the far side of the pens. By now the mist had lifted from the hillside leading to the loading platform. Below, toward the river, the countryside remained shrouded as before. Waller and Tarpley expected Willie to make his move from that direction. Instead Willie crept slowly, carefully toward the house. He finally opened a side window and slipped inside.

"Lord, here's another one," one of the ladies cried in alarm.

"No, that's Mr. Fletcher," a dark-haired boy told them. "He's come to help us."

"Oh, Mr. Fletcher, we're so glad to see you," the taller of the women said. She wore an apron coated with flour, and Willie decided she must be the cook. The other was certainly Mrs. Ross.

"Get the little ones over behind that counter," Willie

instructed as he approached the door. Outside Waller and Tarpley shouted taunts and curses. Even now they expected Willie to rise out of the fog and fight it out. Instead, Willie cracked open the door, took aim, then fired a single shot that shattered Ben Tarpley's left wrist.

"God help me!" Tarpley shouted, stumbling forward. "I'm shot!"

Waller instantly darted toward a nearby boxcar and escaped. Willie kicked the wall in frustration. Tarpley, on the other hand, was clearly in a bad way.

"Come on, Fletcher!" Tarpley called. "Finish it. You've shot my arm half off, but I'm still game. I've got a gun. I can shoot. Come on, you devil!"

Willie crept back to the window, then motioned toward the women.

"When I go back out the window, somebody open the door. Stay clear, though. Tarpley's bound to shoot."

Mrs. Ross nodded, motioned for her young son to stay under cover, and took station beside the door.

Willie nodded, then crawled through the window as she opened the door. Tarpley rose to his feet and fired wildly. Willie took aim at the crippled gunman, then shot twice. The first bullet spun Tarpley around in a circle, and the second slammed into his hip. The killer fumbled with his pistol a moment, then aimed in Willie's direction.

"You're out of chances," Willie mumbled as he fired the Winchester again. This time the bullet smashed Tarpley's cheek. Tarpley's head snapped back, then dropped forward as his legs gave way.

"Ben?" Waller shouted from the boxcar.

"He's finished!" Willie yelled in answer. "Now it's your turn."

Waller didn't linger at the freight car. Instead he turned and sought refuge in the fog-covered embankment. Willie passed the nervous longhorns, then stepped back to the door of the house.

"Get out of here," he told the former captives. "They may have friends about."

"Be careful, Mr. Fletcher," young Donny Ross called. The others nodded their agreement, and Mrs. Ross promised to pray for his safety.

"You best concern yourselves with getting home," Willie cautioned them. "Tell the marshal he needn't worry anymore about Ben Tarpley."

Waller was another matter, though. As Willie headed toward the river, he took care to listen for sounds of movement. The mist provided a perfect shield, and Waller was plenty capable of turning the tables on Wil Fletcher or anyone else too careless to watch his step.

The sound of someone splashing through the shallows of the river attracted Willie's attention, and he made his way slowly toward the distant embankment. He wished he knew Waller better, had some idea where Macpherson might be. Perhaps the stockmen had gathered near the river. Any moment a gang of horsemen might arrive.

As it happened, no such salvation awaited Zac Waller. The fog began to drift away, and Willie watched with satisfaction as the naked bank of the Arkansas revealed itself. Perhaps a mile to the west a wagon stood watch on the crossing. North of there the Whitman farmhouse hosted a few lingering cowboys. Beside the river, hidden from view by a pile of boulders, cowered Zac Waller. The gunfighter turned bushwhacker was totally concealed. Only the barrel of a rifle gave away his position.

"I'll be down for you in a bit, Waller!" Willie called. "I see you down in those rocks. Won't be much longer."

Waller made no movement, and for an instant Willie wondered if the rifle barrel might not be a clever ruse to lure Willie in that direction. Soon the barrel moved slightly, though, and a flash of red fabric betrayed Waller's presence.

"Come on down, Fletcher!" Waller finally yelled.

"Can't stay up on that embankment forever. I've got help coming, you know."

"Do you now?" Willie answered. "I think not. Don't despair, though. I'll be along by and by. I kind of enjoy this game. It's a bit like playing a wise old catfish. You've got the hook in your gullet, Waller. I don't mind letting it tear at you awhile."

Waller muttered a curse. Willie laughed. Then a twig snapped on the far side of the embankment, and Willie swung his rifle in that direction.

"Hold up there!" Thom MacKay cried out as Willie raised the Winchester. "I'm on your side, remember?"

"Just about got yourself shot in half," Willie said, waving the marshal over. "You've got to be crazy coming down here like that."

"I promised to watch your back, remember? Could hardly do that from Main Street."

"Waller's down in those rocks," Willie explained. "I thought to wait him out. If he doesn't come out of his hole, I'll go down and get him a little later. No point to rushing it."

"You've grown smarter."

"It's the way you grow old in this business."

"In mine, too."

Willie sprawled out along the crest of the embankment and sighed. There was only the waiting left now. MacKay knew that, too. So did Zac Waller.

After half an hour, Waller made a move toward escape. He got less than a foot before Willie raised the Winchester and fired.

"Hang it, Fletcher!" Waller yelled in dismay. "Don't you ever sleep?"

"I'll sleep just fine the day after you hang," Willie replied.

"I'll never hang," Waller declared. "I've seen too many

165

men drop short. Sometimes you find the hangman doesn't know what he's about. The rope's too long, and the poor fool thrashes around."

"I'll bring Josh Berry out from Hays!" MacKay promised. "He knows the business."

"So, you've got the marshal with you, eh? He payin' you, Fletcher? What have you made on this deal, twenty, fifty dollars? I've got three hundred you can have just for givin' me a three-hour start."

"That's not much of an offer," Willie said. "Seems to me your hide would be worth a thousand easy."

"Three hundred's all I got. I'd send you the rest."

Willie laughed, and Waller fired in the direction of the sound.

"Don't shoot up all your shells, Waller!" MacKay warned.

"You tin-star marshals!" Waller yelled. "I know you well enough. You think you can take the three hundred off me once I'm dead. I'll burn it first."

A trickle of smoke rose from behind the rocks, and Willie couldn't help smiling at the notion of Waller burning the bank notes. How could a man like Zac Waller, one who'd lived and died for the jingle of a twenty-dollar gold piece, understand money had nothing to do with it? The flames spread, and Willie watched in alarm as he realized the grass had caught fire. For a moment it seemed the embankment might turn into an inferno. Then the wind shifted, and the flames turned back toward the river.

"No!" Waller screamed as the smoke roared down on him like some belching dragon. "No!"

In desperation Waller took his rifle and made a desperate rush toward the river. Willie took a deep breath and fired. The bullet tore through Waller's thigh, and the gunman fell into the shallows. The flames rushed closer, and Waller screamed in terror. Willie and MacKay wove their way cautiously down the hillside. They discovered Zac

166

Waller in the river, one arm frantically drowning the flames that still crept up his shoulder.

Willie stamped out the edge of the brushfire, then dragged Waller to shore. The outlaw's chest and legs were burned black, and he cried in agony.

"Know a doc who'd like to take a look at me?" Waller asked as he groaned. Blood continued to seep from a torn artery in his leg.

"There was one till you shot him," Willie replied bitterly.

"Doesn't matter," Waller said, wincing as he grabbed his bleeding leg. "It'd be a waste to go to all that trouble just so you could hang me. I could use a drink, though."

"We'll get you up the hill," MacKay said, kicking Waller's rifle away.

"Why bother?" Waller asked. "I know what you want. I won't tell you."

"Tell us what?" Willie asked.

"Mac. I won't give him up."

"Why would we want him?" MacKay asked.

"You know he's the one sent us after the doc, had Reed shoot that kid deputy. We'd have had you last night, Fletcher, only that fool of a boy, Hobbs, told us the wrong room. Killed ourselves the wrong man."

"You hear that clear, Wil?" MacKay asked. "I'd call that a deathbed confession. If we can't hang this one, we'll sure have a fine party for Macpherson."

"Will you?" Waller asked, coughing. He turned to one side, and Willie shoved MacKay clear. Waller drew a small pistol from a back pocket, but before he could take aim, Willie fired his Colt through the outlaw's chest.

MacKay got to his feet and stared down at Waller. The dying gunman's eyes opened wide, then glazed over as he coughed out his life.

"He was a slippery one," Willie said, replacing his pistol in its holster. "Now there's only Macpherson to attend to."

"That'll be easy enough now," MacKay said, grinning. "No judge in creation could ignore what we just heard."

Willie nodded, then turned and started back toward town. It was fine for MacKay to envision courtrooms and trials. Willie knew it would be settled elsewhere.

CHAPTER 19

Macpherson was gone. He'd simply vanished. He left nary a hint as to his whereabouts. He continued to elude justice, in spite of Thom MacKay's every effort.

No cattle herds came to Edwards now. There were no riders sent south to draw them to town, and the saloons were boarded closed by the Citizens' Committeemen. When the last of the longhorns were nudged aboard freight cars headed eastward, the buyers left payment with Marshal Thom MacKay.

"If he was still in Kansas, he would have found a way to collect this money," MacKay said, showing the stack of bank notes to Willie. The marshal paid off the few stockmen remaining at the pens, then watched the crew mount up and head for Dodge City. They were followed by the last of the cowboys and a single Kansas City buyer.

"I believe it's finally over," MacKay observed.

"Maybe," Willie said less confidently. "But there's still Rufe Macpherson."

Willie said more or less the same thing when he sat with Les Cobb that same afternoon on the porch of the Trent house. The doctor continued to limp badly, but Les was getting up and about rather well now.

"Let it go, Willie," Les urged. "It's a job for the law. Thom'll find him. We'll handle it."

"You think I should leave, don't you? Just ride off and forget who it was that brought all this grief down on us? He's not gone, Les. This was his dream. Not everyone can run out on his dream, you know. A man like Macpherson, one who's come so close, isn't likely to make it this easy."

"He's not one to risk jail, either. All this time he's hidden behind Ballinger and those toughs from the stockyards. Now he hasn't even sent word to the people who run his shops. The mercantile's closed. Half the town's boarded up and deserted. Even the girls down at the river have hitched their wagons and taken off for Dodge."

"He's nearby, Les. I can feel him."

Les only shook his head and smiled.

As the days passed, frustrated townspeople began taking a personal vengeance on Rufus Macpherson. Stores and shops were cleared of goods. Barrels of beer and bottles of whiskey were dumped into the Arkansas River. Finally, a mob of citizens gathered at the stockyards and began setting the deserted cattle pens ablaze.

"Looks like dreams burn well," Les remarked to Willie as they sat together on Ellen's porch and stared at the rising cloud of smoke.

"It must be eating away at him," Willie said, staring off into the distance.

"You still think he's around, don't you?"

"Where else would he go?"

"Thom's ridden half the county," Les said, shaking his head. "There are farmers and teamsters around who'd love to send Macpherson to the hangman. He must be a magician to avoid them all."

"Maybe he is."

"You just can't let loose of it, can you?"

"Call it Texas stubborn. I never was much good at letting go."

"You let go of Ellie."

"Yes," Willie said, looking off down the street. "That was different, though. With her, it was like I'd caught a butterfly. She was so bright and beautiful, too bright and beautiful to tie to the kind of life I would have given her. That's why I asked you and Trav to tell her I was dead, so she could find someone better."

"You never found anybody else?"

"No."

"Are you sure it's not Ellie that's holding you here?"

"Maybe it is. I tell myself I have to deal with Macpherson because he can still bring her harm. If he was dangling from a rope, though, I'd have to be on my way."

"You could stay. Someone's got to run the mercantile, operate the bank and the feed store."

"Can you see me selling stick candy to children and flour to farmers? No, I'm not one to take to towns. I'll be off soon."

"Where?"

"Does it matter? One place is as good as another."

"I got a letter from Trav. He says you spoke with a neighbor of his, Ted Slocum. There's land down on the Clear Fork perfect for running horses."

"I'll never go back to Texas," Willie said, swallowing a bitterness that filled his thoughts. "Maybe I'll try the high country again. I found peace there once."

"Peace doesn't come from a place, Willie."

"I know. It comes with forgetting. And that comes hard."

He left Les on the porch and started back toward the hotel. As he passed the mercantile, though, a young woman of twenty or so reached out and took his arm.

"Hello," she said, blinking her painted eyes. Her dress

171

was scarlet and white, an odd combination. The lace cuffs marked her as one of Macpherson's harlots. Willie shook loose her fingers and stepped away.

"I thought you'd all left," he told her.

"Not all," she said, laughing. "We've still done a fair business down at the Sundown . . . Hotel."

"Oh?"

"You never came out that way, though. Why is that?"

"I've been busy."

"So I hear. They call you Fletcher, I understand."

"That's right."

"I'm Anna. I was Abigail in Wichita, Venus in Dodge. I've had cause to change my name, too."

"And?"

"I came to get you. He's waiting for you."

"Who?"

"Rufe," she said somberly. "Says there's business to settle. He'd rather take it up with you than the marshal."

"There's talk of putting up a reward. You might make a better bargain with MacKay."

"I'm not doing this for money," she said angrily. "Rufe's been a friend. He knows what's waiting. He isn't begging any favors off you. He's a fair man, Rufe is. He's been more than good to me and the girls, but we can't live on dreams and promises. Neither can he. The money's gone, and he's grown tired."

"What's he want from me?"

She looked away a minute, and Willie felt a chill come over him. She was fighting to hold back a tear. Working cattle towns left women hard, and he'd known few fancy women who could cry over a man.

"Just me?" he asked her.

"I'm to tell the others, too, in time. But you first."

"Why?"

"You'll have to ask him," she said, walking away.

"Wait," Willie called. "Where will I find him?"

"At the Sundown. Take the road out from town, headed west. It's an old farmhouse. You can't miss it."

No, Willie thought as he watched her go. It's the old Whitman place. Somehow it was fitting that Macpherson's final refuge should be a house filled with false love, inhabited by deceit and broken promises.

It was a most peculiar message carried by a most unusual messenger. But perhaps it was because of it that Willie headed to the livery and saddled his horse. Old Thunder responded with an eagerness that raised Willie's spirits. The horse had been too long in a stable. Willie wasn't the only one ready to return to the freedom of open country.

He arrived at the Sundown Hotel a little after noon. The place appeared deserted. Ropes had been strung for drying linens. They stood hauntingly bare, empty. Shutters banged against the sides of the house. The door stood ajar. Except for a single mule grazing near the charred embers of the Whitman barn, not even so much as a prairie dog could be seen.

Willie drew his Colt and started for the front door. He cautiously swung the door open wide, then darted inside. He discovered a candle burning on a small table in the sitting room. Rufus Macpherson sat in a single chair next to the table, his face strangely hollow as if from lack of food and rest.

"So, it's you," Macpherson mumbled. "I'm glad. I thought it might be the marshal, or even Trent. Anna's always been true to her word, but by now there could be money involved. She's a fair businesswoman."

"What do you want?" Willie asked.

"Have a drink?"

"You brought me here for a purpose."

"Sure I did, but is there harm in having a sip of whiskey in the meanwhile? Call it courtesy to the loser."

Macpherson drew out a bottle of Irish whiskey. A third

at best remained. He poured Willie a glass, then took a long sip from the bottle.

"You've been here all along. Thom MacKay will be disappointed he didn't find you before," Willie said.

"The girls are used to keeping secrets."

"So why give in now?"

"Didn't seem much use in playing out the hand when there were no new cards to be drawn."

Willie followed Macpherson's eyes toward the river. Smoke from the blazing stockyards stained the horizon even now.

"I never understood why you chose Edwards," Willie said, sipping the whiskey. "Never made sense. You could've gone a few miles to the west, built your own town."

"Sounds so simple," Macpherson muttered. "The best crossing of the Arkansas is here. Besides, I thought Edwards would jump at the chance to be another Dodge City. Simple! Life's that way sometimes. A cut of the cards. Sometimes you think you've got a handful of aces, and they turn out to be treys over deuces."

"Sometimes," Willie agreed.

"Was what I had in mind so bad? Tell me, Fletcher, was my dream so dark that men should have died over it?"

"Men die for strange reasons. Some risk their hide for a few greenbacks. Others, like young Ty Green, die for an ideal."

"And you?"

"I don't die," Willie said, finishing the whiskey. "I just go on."

"Nobody lives forever, though. I never thought much about it before, but we all go in time. Me? I imagined I'd rest on a tall hill overlooking a town that took my name. Now they want to hang me, let the little children dance while I dangle from a rope. And for what?"

"Pride maybe. There are empty sections west of here.

174

But you had to have a town, this town. And when the people stood up to you, you struck them down. There's a price to pay for murder."

"You're the last man on earth to preach to me about murder, Fletcher. How many have you killed?"

"Too many," Willie said, nodding as he stepped toward the door. "Thom MacKay will be here soon. He'll see you have a trial."

"Trial?" Macpherson asked. "No, that won't happen. Care to try your luck?"

Macpherson reached inside his coat, and Willie swung his Colt toward the haggard man's head.

"Just cards," Macpherson explained. "Hundred dollars a hand. What do you say? Help pass the time."

"All right," Willie agreed, reluctantly sitting across the table as Macpherson refilled the glass with whiskey before dealing two hands.

"How many?" the dealer asked.

Willie frowned. He had a worthless collection of cards. He kept a ten and seven of spades and asked for three. Macpherson took three himself.

"I'd raise you another hundred," Macpherson said, "only I don't have it. So all I can do is call."

"A pair of sevens," Willie announced, turning over his cards. He'd managed to draw the seven of hearts along with a trey and a five.

"Pair of sevens," Macpherson grumbled. "Cleaned out by a pair of fool sevens."

Macpherson tossed his cards toward the window, then handed over a single, crisp hundred-dollar bank note.

"It's time I was leaving now," Willie announced.

"Not just yet," Macpherson said, stumbling to his feet. "You haven't tended to all your business."

"Yes, I have," Willie said, backing his way toward the door.

"No!" Macpherson said, setting a loaded Colt on the table. "On the count of five."

"I'm finished with this!" Willie shouted. "I've had enough."

"Enough?" Macpherson cried, pointing toward the smoke. "You've killed me already. You've taken it all. You wouldn't leave a horse with a broken leg to suffer! At least let me die like a man, not a cow gone to the slaughterhouse. You think I could face all those laughing fools?"

"You never shot a man face-to-face," Willie said, his eyes growing cold. "You did your murder like a bookkeeper, picked out a name here and there, paid for it like you paid for a plank for the mercantile or a pane of glass. Killing steals part of a man away."

"Do it! On five!"

"No," Willie said, slipping through the door before Macpherson had a chance to fire.

"Damn you, Fletcher! Come back!"

Macpherson fired through the door, and Willie dove to the ground. Silence engulfed them for a moment. Then there was a third, muffled shot. Macpherson groaned and fell to the floor.

"It's for the best," Thom MacKay said when he arrived an hour later. "I never cared much for hangings."

"Me, neither," Willie agreed.

"I'll send word to Jonas Wheeler in Dodge. There'll be plenty of money for a proper funeral once we sell off the property. I think the burial ought to be in Dodge, too. There are those who wouldn't want him in the churchyard here. Somebody dug up Reed Ballinger and threw him in the river."

Willie turned and stared westward.

"You were right," MacKay went on. "Macpherson was here all along. I guess when the stockyards burned, he knew it was over."

"It was over the day Jack Trent forced Ballinger to back down," Willie said, kicking a rock across the farmyard.

"No, it was when you killed Ballinger. Won't end that way much longer, though. The law's taking over. Ballinger's kind grow scarcer each year."

My kind, too, Willie thought.

"Given any more thought to the future?" MacKay asked. "That fool Les Cobb plans to stay on as sheriff here. I need a deputy more than ever."

"I'm no marshal," Willie said, laughing.

"What are you then? A rancher?"

"I don't know for sure," Willie admitted. "A memory. A shadow. Who knows?"

"I've got to head back for Hays soon. Care to ride along, say, as far as Dodge?"

"No, I've got my eyes set on another direction. And there are good-byes to say."

"I wish you luck, Wil Fletcher. Or Delamer. Or whatever it will be this time," the marshal said, shaking Willie's hand.

"And I you, Thom MacKay. Watch yourself."

"I always do," MacKay said, laughing to himself. "I always do."

CHAPTER 20

Willie rode back to town slowly. From time to time he'd wander off to some hill or another. He'd pause long enough to watch a pair of farm boys fishing a creek or catch a glimpse of the stage headed west from Edwards. Willie had an impulse to nudge Thunder into a gallop and chase that coach to California. Approaching town, he lost the urge. For so long a time Ellen had been lost to him. Her gentle touch and soothing words would be missed more than ever before. And yet he knew he could not stay. What could he be to her now? A memory? An embarrassment? Sooner or later she'd come to be sorry he'd appeared.

He left Thunder with the livery boy and headed down the street to the hotel. The schoolhouse was alive with children's laughter. Sarah Henshaw was sweeping the church steps, and a boy who reminded Willie far too much of Ty Green was polishing the windows of the jailhouse.

I'll bet they've already scrubbed the bloodstains from the carpets at the hotel, Willie thought. It was strange how fast people could erase those last months from memory. Willie could never forget that quickly.

"Hear the news?" someone down the street shouted.

"Marshal MacKay's bringing in Rufe Macpherson. He's dead!"

"Good for the marshal," another added.

Willie ignored them and strode through the open door of the hotel. He nodded to Wheaton, then climbed the stairs and sauntered along to his room. It took but a few moments to gather his meager belongings and descend the stairway.

"You're not leaving?" Wheaton asked when Willie handed over his key.

"Little point to staying. Macpherson's finished. It's time to move on."

"I thought maybe you'd hang around till Sheriff Cobb was better."

"You don't need me now," Willie said, glancing at the shotgun resting even now behind the front desk. "You and your committee can handle things just fine."

"Is it that easy for you to go?"

"Easy?" Willie asked, his fingers trembling as he drew a line through his name on the register. "It's never easy. But it's time. How much do I owe you?"

"I figure I owe you. I never paid you for those cabinets."

"Oh? You picked up my feed bill, and there's the damage upstairs to take into account."

"That's not your doing. You know, there's still a good deal of carpentry work to be had in Edwards. I'd recommend you highly."

"No, it's better I leave."

"Where will you go?"

"West probably. I passed a good autumn up on the Powder River once."

"Sioux are swarming all over that country."

"They won't be for long. The Army'll see to that."

"Most likely. Ever been to Cheyenne, up in the Wyoming Territory?"

"Rode through there once."

"I've got a brother runs freight between there and Green River. He's always looking for a man that knows horses. I could send him a wire, have him extend a welcoming hand to you."

"To Wil Fletcher?" Willie asked, laughing. "I'll likely be somebody else by the time I clear Kansas."

"If you happen by, tell him you're the carpenter from Edwards. He'll know you from my wire."

Willie nodded, but inside he wondered how it was possible for Wheaton's brother to know a man who didn't know himself.

"You'll keep an eye on Ellen and the little ones?" Willie asked.

"Sure, but Jack's not likely to be lame for long. Les is about, too. And the boys, shoot, they'll likely be up in the Medicine Bow country, hunting buffalo with you in a year or two."

"If there are any left," Willie said sadly.

"Watch the trail ahead of you, Wil."

"Sure," Willie said as he slung his blanket roll over one shoulder and turned toward the door. He knew, though, that it was the trail behind that merited watching.

Willie then made his way to the livery. The boy had brushed Thunder's coat to a sheen, and the horse greeted its owner with an eager bellow.

"Not long now, boy," Willie said, stroking the horse's nose. "We'll soon be back on the plain."

"I brushed him good," the stable boy said. Willie smiled, then tossed the youngster a silver dollar. The boy brightened like a Christmas candle, then brought Willie's blanket and saddle over.

"Thanks," Willie said as he set the blanket across Thunder's broad back. "You've done a good job looking after him, son. What's left is for me to do."

The boy nodded, then trotted over to tend the other

horses. As Willie set the saddle in place and tightened the cinch, he heard someone enter the stable. He detected a scent of rosewater and molasses.

"Ellie?" he whispered.

"I heard you were down here. They brought Macpherson in. Did you . . ."

"No, he did it himself," Willie explained. "Couldn't face the pain, I suppose."

"The pain?"

"Of losing his dream. It's as bad as a man can feel."

"You talk as if you know."

"I do," Willie said, draping the bridle over Thunder's nose. "I've buried a few dreams in my time."

"You talk as if you were ancient. You're not yet thirty."

"That's a lifetime in my line of work."

"You could change that."

"I've tried. It's not that easy."

"Where will you go?"

"North. West. Wherever this big black horse sets his feet. One place is pretty much the same as another. Wheaton says he's got a brother running freight up in Wyoming. That's nice country. I might try my hand at that."

"There's a place for you here."

"As what? Somebody's spare uncle? Oh, Ellie, we had some fine times once, and you'll never be far from my heart. You know that. But you've got a husband, a family . . ."

"I feel like I've found something I lost long ago, Willie. You never were much good at lying. I see how fond you are of the boys, and you scarcely know them. You need us."

"I can't stay," he said, rubbing a tear from his eye. "How could I? I'd sit and watch those boys who might've been my sons grow tall. I couldn't stand being so near . . . knowing . . . that you'd always be too far away."

"Willie?" she called, resting her head on his shoulder.

"I used to dream of finding you again," he whispered. "I never wanted anything half as much. Jack Trent's a good man, though. Better'n me. If I stayed, I'd prove an embarrassment. I'm like an old bull buffalo that's watching his prairie get chewed up by railroads and towns. The herd's dying off, and I'm left behind as a relic of what was here before."

"You're more than that."

"No, and what's worse, I know it. It'd be hard for you to watch me grow old. I'll sour like wasted milk. There's no room in a town for Wil Fletcher."

"What about Willie Delamer?"

"Trav and Les didn't lie when they told you he was dead. He is. Me, I'm just a ghost that keeps popping up, stirring old memories. I'm better forgotten."

"Not by me. I'd remember even if you hadn't come down here and saved our lives, our town. I missed you before, Willie. It will be twice as bad now."

"No, you'll pick up the pieces and rebuild your life. You'll replace the broken glass and putty the holes in the walls. You'll mend the curtains and patch the furniture."

"And you?"

"I'll just go on."

"Promise you'll come back sometime? Visit?"

"My life's rarely brought me back anywhere I've been before, Ellie. I never like to make promises I can't keep."

"Willie?" she cried as he pulled away and climbed atop Thunder. "Don't go. You've not said good-bye to the little ones. William's just leaving the schoolhouse about now, and Jack will want to . . ."

"I never was one for farewells," he said, reaching down to lift her chin. "It's hard heading out sometimes, but I'll always rest easier knowing you're faring well."

"Willie!"

He touched her hand a final time, then nudged Thunder

182

into a trot. He never looked back, for the sight of her tear-streaked face might have rent his heart in two.

"Carry me on the west wind, boy," Willie whispered as Thunder stepped briskly through Edwards, past the hotel and the jail, by Ellen's house, across the railroad tracks, and along to where the ashes of Macpherson's stockyards scarred the landscape. "Now, Thunder, go!" he yelled, and the tall black stallion broke into a gallop. He'd race the afternoon sun across the heavens, and the Rockies would be his far horizon.

Don't cry too long for me, Ellie, he silently told the clouds as if they might carry the message to her. For leaving is the thing I do best and most often.

And perhaps, fate being what it was, a better place and a kinder world lay ahead.

ABOUT THE AUTHOR

G. Clifton Wisler comes by his interest in the West natu-
rally. Born in Oklahoma and raised in Texas, he discovered
early on a fascination for the history of the region. His first
novel, MY BROTHER, THE WIND, received a nomina-
tion for the American Book Award in 1980. Among the
many others that have followed are THUNDER ON THE
TENNESSEE, winner of the Western Writers of America
Spur Award for Best Western Juvenile Novel of 1983;
WINTER OF THE WOLF, a Spur finalist in 1982; and
Delamer Westerns THE TRIDENT BRAND, STARR'S
SHOWDOWN, PURGATORY, ABREGO CANYON, and
THE WAYWARD TRAIL. In addition to his writing,
Wisler frequently speaks to school groups and conducts
writing clinics. He lives in Garland, Texas, where he is
active in the Boy Scouts.

G. CLIFTON WISLER

************ *presents* ************

THE BEST OF THE WEST